I0682624

eloquent corpse

by Audrey Lavin

Copyright © 2007 by Audrey Lavin

No part of this work may be reproduced or transmitted in any form unless expressly permitted by Federal copyright law or with written permission from the author or publisher.

Printed in the United States of America

ISBN 978-0-6151-7351-1

Library of Congress Control Number: 2007940463

$11.95

CAVE HORSE PRESS
Dover, Ohio

DEDICATION

This book is dedicated with love to my family:

Carl, Sr.
Maud, David, Krister, and Amanda
Carl, Lauren, Austin, Seth, Carter, and Celeste
Franklin, Ann, Abby, Nat, and Liz
Douglas, Lisa, Simone, and Eleanor

Acknowledgements:

With deep appreciation to all of those who have helped Mary Beth and Tony solve their second mystery:

"They are the charming gardeners who make our souls blossom."
　　　　　　　　　—Marcel Proust

To my family for emotional and editorial encouragement: Maud Lavin, Carl and Lauren Lavin, Franklin, Ann, and Abby Lavin, Douglas Lavin and Lisa Greenwald, and to Carl H. Lavin, Sr, encourager extraordinaire.

To the Wednesday Writing Workshop and the Akron Ms. Club for shared laughter and informed analysis.

To the many friends whose suggestions have been used to round out characters, places, and plot, with special thanks to James A. Bower, architect; Ernie Campbell, MCSE; Dan T. Chrzanowski, cover designer; Charita Goshay, columnist and feature writer; Eric Haas, BS, NREMT-P; Gordon Maupin, Executive Director, The Wilderness Center; Joseph McLaughlin, publisher; Rich Reding, owner and manager of the Lynn Drive-In Theater; Doug Savage, writer; Caroline Totten, writer; and to Lisa Ohlweiler, photographer, for author's photo.

PROLOGUE

"There are four kinds of homicide:
felonious, excusable, justifiable, and praiseworthy."

—Ambrose Bierce

Chapter One

Sunday night & Monday morning

"Tomorrow, tomorrow . . . " Mary Beth Goldberg, the youngest of the writers invited to "Ohio Creates," sang smugly, though slightly off-key. In the privacy of her room at Prince George House, she hummed the rest of the song's forgotten words while optimistically adding up the pluses of spending a week in Lakeville, Ohio.

The biggest plus (handsomest, too) was Hans, the writer she had met earlier through a parking lot accident. Though the afternoon's meet-and-greet had been as competitive as a wrestling match, Sunday night dinner, seated next to Hans, had been enjoyable. He seemed interested and might be more than interesting. *He's even famous*, she thought. She mentally jabbed herself. Of course, her real purpose in attending the workshop was to advance her writing career. Keep that goal front and center, Mary Beth, would be her motto.

As she put on her pajamas, she continued to chastise herself for thinking of Hans so much. She was supposed to have a boyfriend if not a fiancé. Tony's letter was in her back pocket. She opened it. "It's O.K. to kiss a fool. It's O.K. to let a fool kiss you. But it's not O.K. to be fooled by a kiss." *How does he know what I'm thinking*, she wondered. *Anyway, why am I feeling guilty? When I got the invite to "Ohio Creates," he was the one who said, "Let's stretch it to two weeks; a little time apart might be a good idea."*

Mary Beth allowed herself to think for a minute, but only a minute, of Tony Bartlett's quirky good looks, his rangy 6'2" frame, and the way he had quit his creative engineering research job to follow her to

Midfield College Campus in Ohio. *Stop. I'm not in Lakeville to think about Tony.* She pulled herself back to the here and now, to thoughts of her first day at Prince George House. *Most important,* she thought, *I didn't make one catty remark about that overly kittenish writer, Clara.* She laughed at her own slight joke and promptly fell asleep.

A quick shower on awakening early Monday morning gave Mary Beth a chance to inspect herself for what turned out to be non-existent bruise marks from Sunday's tackle by Hans. She put on fresh jeans and her take-me-seriously black turtle-neck before running a brush through her swimmer-friendly haircut. The mirror showed her the cut and color were as becoming as they were practical. Beside, she liked thinking of herself as a "dirty blonde."

With the creak of the stair treads betraying her eagerness, Mary Beth almost skipped down them at 7 a. m. She was conscious of starting a new adventure. And there was Hans, waiting for her.

"Good morning, Mary Beth," he greeted her with a smile and a slight tap to her wrist-watch. "Seven o'clock. Are you always this punctual?

"Notoriously punctual. Ask my students."

Realizing that the unstated sub-text of their mutual attraction was present in each of her conventional conversations with Hans, Mary Beth dared a little and added, "I hope knowing that I'll be on time doesn't take any of the mystery away from me, or, I mean, away from things. Responsible people still have fun."

Then she retreated and found much to discuss about breakfast.

The mystery writing team of Sara and Clara were next on the scene giving each other significant looks as they noted Hans and Mary Beth sitting together, talking more than they were eating.

Mary Beth sat facing the buffet. She could hear Clara actually asking for milk instead of tea or coffee. *This was carrying the feline resemblance too far.*

Clara was making her own sharp observations of the two seated writers, *Were their knees touching? Was something going on already?*

Sara nudged her, mid-speculation, pointing to the platters of Danish on the table. "Did you get that Architecture 101 lecture last night from Hans about the Danish Prince George marrying Queen Anne when she ascended the throne? How far are we going to carry this Queen Anne-style house theme?" she asked as she piled up her plate with one of each flavor.

Just before the dining room's 9 a.m. announced closing time, hosts Malcolm and Nikki Haverford entered with Buck, all desperately seeking coffee. In keeping with his cowboy persona, Buck was leathered up, sporting a suede fringed vest and highly decorated, calfskin cowboy boots

"I swear he just hitched up his gun-belt," Mary Beth whispered to Hans.

"You're right," he replied, touching her shoulder in agreement. "Have you noticed what an oddly costumed crew "Ohio Creates" has attracted? I'll bet our co-authors Sara and Clara think a 'wardrobe malfunction' is a sweater without a cat on it!"

Nikki interrupted Mary Beth's laugh-out-loud response. "Looks like the gang's all here," she chirped weakly trying to cheer up the group. Even Nikki was aware that Malcolm's introductory speech had fallen flat the previous evening.

"Not Marian," someone said.

Excuses were offered:

"She said she was feeling a little weak and sick to the stomach last night, so she's 'sleeping in' as we Ohioans say."

"Maybe she doesn't eat breakfast. It's a meal many people skip.

"Oh, my doctor says that . . .

"Marian always eats breakfast" came the identical interruption from Malcolm, Hans, and Buck in almost perfect chorus. The ensuing shades of red that suffused their faces were not as evenly matched and ranged from slowly rising pink realization, to bright red acknowledgement, to great purple blotches of anger at self-betrayal.

Malcolm had moved next to Mary Beth and Hans. "I'm especially pleased that the two of you are here," he murmured, physically and conversationally distancing himself from the subject of Marian.

"I feel that I know you both deeply. Your writing and my art are similar. They are in a state of becoming."

A state of becoming? Mary Beth added that to Malcolm's remark Sunday night about their being "one under the skin." Her soul grimaced. She turned away, choosing to join the general conversation. "I think I'll go knock on Marian's door," she interjected. "If the news being bruited about this breakfast table is true, if 'Marian does always eat breakfast,' she won't mind my waking her."

Hans followed Mary Beth as she headed upstairs. Sara trooped along. Clara, determining not to climb those creaky stairs one more time than she had to, went on eating her Danishes.

Nikki trailed Malcolm, who was headed away from the stairwell toward their office. She made one final announcement before she left the dining room, "There'll be hot coffee put out for Marian and anyone else who wants it."

Buck's disapproval of Hans, Sara, and Mary Beth's quest was mumbled in a diatribe heard only by Clara, "What's the matter with you people? I wouldn't want to be disturbed and I'm not going to be the one to disturb any ol' gal, especially Marian. She has one helluva temper in the morning. Let her amble in when she wants to."

By then, Mary Beth was knocking on the door to bedroom #1. It had been labeled the "Longfellow Room" by the Haverfords who had given Prince George House an historical and literary aura by naming all of their bedrooms after famous authors, authors who had definitely never slept there.

When Marian didn't respond to the initial knocks, Mary Beth tried the doorknob. The door was locked. Hans said, "You're too gentle, Mary Beth." He reached over her head, partially to (accidentally) brush against her, partially to pick up the tempo by pounding on the door lintel. No response from Marian. A slight flush of warmth from Mary Beth.

After a few more minutes without any sound coming from the other side of the transom, four minds had a simultaneous flash. Sara was the first to ask if anyone had a cell phone. Mary Beth and Hans produced theirs. But none of the highly intelligent group knew the phone number of Prince George House, and Information didn't respond. The proffered cell phones were pronounced useless. Hans said, "I'll go down to the desk. Nikki can use the inter-house line and call Marian from there. You girls might as well wait here."

Girls? thought Mary Beth annoyed. *Girls?* thought Sara pleased.

A few minutes after Hans left them, they could hear the phone start to ring in the room. And ring. It was still ringing when Hans reappeared. Nikki, complete with her chain of numbered room keys, was at his side. "Marian is hopefully deeply asleep," Nikki said, "but I'm going in to see."

Hans touched Mary Beth's arm as he suggested to Nikki,"I think you should take one other woman with you as a precautionary measure.

"O.K., Mary Beth, here we go," Nikki said as she turned the heavy metal key in the lock. Nikki looked over her shoulder at Mary Beth, who reassured her, "This really is the best way to address the issue." The women entered the oppressively floral room almost together. Hans and Sara were too curious to wait. With an interchange of understanding nods, they followed a few steps behind the appointed search party.

And there was Marian sitting up in bed with a book in front of her. She looked almost happy with her mouth twisted into a slightly sardonic smile. But her brilliant red lipstick stood out too conspicuously against the paleness of her skin. Still, every platinum hair was jelled into place and, (*leave it to Marian*, Mary Beth thought) she was wearing what looked like a brand new La Perla night-gown. "Who goes to bed like that?" Mary Beth involuntarily asked out loud.

"I'm afraid it has to be someone who is dead," Hans replied as he approached the bed, now ahead of Mary Beth. "Look at her coloring—or lack of." He didn't realize that his own face, bleached by shock, was almost as white.

Screams from Sara and shudders from Mary Beth followed, but not much sadness was visible in anyone's eyes as they realized what Hans had said was true.

Mary Beth flashed back to the only other time she had seen a dead body. It had been in the English department at the College. But this was different. That body, Les's, was surrounded by blood, "eloquent blood." She couldn't see any blood in Marian's room. It had to be an unfortunate, but natural, death.

Nikki took one look, assessed the situation, and did what any good hostess would do in an emergency. "I'll make some tea," she said and went downstairs again to do just that.

Mary Beth and Hans flipped open their cell phones again, moving in tandem toward the better reception offered by the balcony. This time the phones were useful. Both callers reached 9-1-1 at about the same time and took turns giving information. Hans reported the death, then paused while Mary Beth added her amateur diagnosis, "I think it was a heart attack."

As soon as she fumbled her cell back into her pocket, Mary Beth began to wonder about the situation. With a shock, the observant writer in her realized that she could no longer sustain her camel wrestling metaphor for the writers' competition; the circumstances now had gone beyond pushing and shoving. She remembered the hostility that had greeted Marian's entrance at the meet-and-greet. *Could looks really kill?*

Chapter Two

Sunday

The camel wrestling imagery had been Mary Beth's direct response to Sunday's meet-and-greet party. *The camel wrestling is over for the afternoon,* she said to herself after the last smile and hand-shake. With an inward grin at her association of ideas, she added *Bring on the clowns—with their shovels.*

She had quickly put a brake on her stream-of-consciousness sarcasm.

Embarrassed, she recalled her own verbal shoving at the party. The "Ohio Creates" conference was bringing out the worst in her. As much as anyone, she had been caught up in the competition of who's-the-most-well-known-writer-at-*this*-conference, even though she knew darn well it wasn't anyone named Professor Mary Beth Goldberg.

A natural comparison with the last writer's conference she'd attended had brought the camel imagery to Mary Beth's mind. It had been two years since that international conference in Izmir, Turkey. Those two years had brought major changes in her life: her relationship with Tony and her job at Midfield Campus College.

"Write On, Professors" had been the title of the Izmir conference. The pun promised fun and stimulation, but the conference didn't deliver. Instead, in a Babel of languages, it delivered a combination of repetitive subject matter and authorial one-upmanship. The final irritant for Mary Beth had been her introduction by the conference chairman. Ignoring her scholarly book on E. M. Forster, he introduced her as "our American guest who is very attractive and unmarried." Mary Beth swore off all literary conferences.

Maybe she should have stayed with her pledge. But with two years to forget the negatives, and the financial incentive of a free ride to "Ohio Creates," plus M.C.C.'s generous faculty enhancement grant, Mary Beth reconsidered. Being the only academic invited to the workshop would be a big plus on her up-coming job evaluation at "McCollege." Getting back into the writing/wrestling game began to seem like a plan.

One positive memory had stayed with her from the Izmir Conference: the splendid afternoon she played hooky. The lecture on "Don't Mail Cookies: Write a Letter to Captivate a Literary Agent," would be a redundancy for Mary Beth and, she had thought, for the entire group of successful, published writers. *Why didn't everyone get up and leave*, she had wondered. Mary Beth did.

So did her new *Ege Üniversitesi* friend, Sechkin Ergun. With a look that emphasized her own distaste, Sechkin had whispered, "Turkey is more fun than this." She had proved it by taking Mary Beth to near-by Ephesus to see the camel wrestling. What had sounded like a poor ethnic joke (camels wrestling?) turned out to be the center of a wonderful day. Mary Beth and Sechkin sat on the hillside with hundreds of Turkish families cooking on their braziers as they all watched the show in the natural amphitheater below them.

Certainly other tourists had been to Ephesus earlier in the weekend to see the famous ruins of the eastern Mediterranean's best preserved classical city. But they obviously had been interested only in early religious relics and the archeology of Roman times. Few had returned to the site to see the ancient wonder that continued as an active sport in contemporary Turkey. When she searched the crowd, Mary Beth couldn't recognize any other western tourist camped on the hillside.

She shared a tarp and food with Sechkin, who had stopped a passing vendor to buy treats. Even now, Mary Beth's mouth watered at the thought of those once unfamiliar pastries, pumpkin sweets and phylo with walnuts. She could still taste the lokmas, those honeyed crisp mini-donuts with the added benefit of having a name she could pronounce. Mary Beth had been fascinated: The top-heavy vendor didn't miss a step on the steep hillside as he worked the crowd balancing his goods in a huge basket on his head.

A special feeling of familial bonding came to her from this participation as observer of the spectacle below and around her. Her ability to blend in was helped by the dark scarf she used to protect her almost-naturally highlighted hair (Sunkissed Blonde #124563) from the Mediterranean sun. The smoke that drifted from the omnipresent charcoal fires and smudged the outlines of individuals completed the visual of her absorption into the group.

It also slightly obscured the dressed-to-kill (not quite literally) camels in the ring below. The wrestling was not bloody or violent. But the camels were naturally pugnacious. The promoters knew what they were doing when they planned the annual camel wrestling for the aggressive, spring rutting season. With their humps covered in jewel-encrusted, flaming red blankets, the camels shoved at each other in round after round like so many Sumo wrestlers, if Sumo wrestlers ever wore muzzles and dressed in flaming red.

Wanting to be close to the gorgeously outfitted, muzzled, drooling camels and their brightly costumed handlers, Mary Beth had gone down into the wrestling rings during intermission. She decided quickly that the wondrous spicy odors rising from the meals being prepared on the surrounding hills were preferable to those emanating from the sweaty camels and climbed back up to find Sechkin and friends she'd run into. She almost missed them in the few recesses left by the ever-darkening sky. Mary Beth, of course, had dropped her disposable camera somewhere on the dark climb up the side of the amphitheater, though she didn't need photographs to remind herself of a day of insight and pleasure, a day that left her with enough metaphors for a lifetime.

But Sunday in Lakeville, Ohio, was worlds away from Izmir, Turkey. Mary Beth reflected on the day. *The camel wrestling is over.* She turned the metaphor around in her mind again, enjoying it as an apt description of that afternoon's cocktail hour. It had been a competitive, but promising opening session to this elite writers' conference at Prince George House in Lakeville.

The attendees who Mary Beth had met at that "Ohio Creates" party were previously known to her only by reputation, though she was familiar with host Malcolm Haverford's art and photography. The other five were writers, and she had tried to read something by each of them before the opening session. The registration list had arrived a week ago, so she'd only gotten as far as a quick read of a children's book by Marian Rogers and a longer stab at finishing the Western romance by H. Buck Carter that had been on *The New York Times* best seller list nine weeks in a row. But *Violent Love Conquers All* wasn't any English Lit Professor's idea of a good read. Mary Beth found Carter's style even cruder than his subject matter. Marian's books had been easily available at Midfield Campus College's bookstore as they were included in kiddie lit courses at the college. Two of Roger's books had been awarded the prestigious John Newberry Medal given each year to the author of the most outstanding children's book. Most university kiddie lit courses now included those two award winners: *Samantha Skips Rope* and *Jared Skips School*. *A fun read*, Mary Beth thought, and I'll be able to tell her so. The infamous Marian will be there.

When Mary Beth had started her drive from Midfield to Lakeville, she had thrown a few of the other authors' books along with her pages of driving directions into her once stylish Coach backpack (an E-Bay find). It sat like some lumpy, inert passenger on the seat next to her, not noticing that it was dropping papers, make-up, and other paraphernalia at every sudden turn or Ohio pot hole.

Driving along the Ohio Turnpike, with one hand on the steering wheel and the other hand feeling through the growing mess, Mary Beth had tried unsuccessfully to find her detailed MapQuest driving directions to Prince George House in Lakeville. She had packed them so carefully. Admitting defeat, she substituted chats with a few friendly gas station attendants for the maps and had no problem finding her destination. It would have taken a specialized sub-set of MapQuest directions to find her way through all of the papers that had fallen on the floor.

So, in spite of her plans having gone awry, she arrived an hour before the 3 p.m. registration time. As she parked her bedazzling blue convertible P.T. Cruiser in front of the huge Victorian house that was to be her live-in conference center for the week, she was happily relieved that for once she wasn't the first. She never could break the habit drummed into her by her parents of always being on time, even in situations where guests were expected to be late. But this afternoon, two other cars were already parked in the circular driveway, a driveway that was large enough to hold a dozen parked cars while (sometime in the house's past) a dozen more could have driven by to deposit elegantly dressed guests at the front door.

The door looked heavy and off-putting. Mary Beth knew instinctively that the original owner had not wanted any unexpected family members or any one else dropping by without an invitation. The house itself, a turreted, castle-like structure with a Midwestern, wrap-around front porch and a balcony projected over it, enchanted her. *To use Henry James's description* (and why wouldn't an English prof quote James?), *this isn't merely a large house; it's truly "a castle of romance."*

Who gave such thought to the detail work? she wondered. *They even used authentic looking bargeboard on the roof to screen the mechanisms necessary for the house's twenty-first century modernization. That house is Victorian and then some.*

Fumbling through her backpack for a camera, Mary Beth added to her mental list of things-to-do, *I'll have to ask if there's a name for this style. Meanwhile, I should take some pictures for my Gothic Lit class. This would be a perfect illustration for the house that James built, the one that's the setting for "The Turn of the Screw."*

audrey lavin

Chapter Three

Sunday, continued

Mary Beth had trouble stepping out of her car to see more of the house. While she had been planning her photo shoot from behind the steering wheel, a Humvee had pulled in close to her, limiting her ability to open her door. Convertibles need extra door-opening space, but that Humvee would have crowded out any thing, any one. Mary Beth unsuccessfully tried to throw her battered backpack out of the door first; it was too lumpy and bulky. Mary Beth wasn't. Scattering a few more papers in the process, she slipped through the opening and stood looking at the elaborate entrance to the house.

She waited, twisting her necklace, the intertwined chains of beads she had bought at the Izmir *souk* two years ago. It had been an intimate, uncovered *souk*, not at all like the huge touristy one in Istanbul. She had followed the maze of tiny streets that started at Konok Square. As she wandered through the market, she stopped to talk and joke with the English-speaking tradesmen in their booths while they tried to sell her their eclectic wares. Beautiful, hand-made gold jewelry was laid out next to cleverly contrived necklaces of native stones and seeds. The elegantly mottled beads she was wearing now had been one of her earliest purchases.

Another had been her "antiquarian" engraved map. In the most helpful of gestures, the dealer had brazenly offered to date the map back to any century she wanted and called on friends conveniently loitering nearby to "verify" the century. Thoughts of the joyous hubbub that ensued still gave Mary Beth a warm glow, as did the "authentic" 18th century map hanging on the living room wall of her white frame rental back in Midfield, Ohio.

As she walked away from her parked car, Mary Beth continued fingering her beads as if they were worry-beads. Seeing the entrance for the first time had made vivid the almost mythical stories she had heard about the Syberstone family and the building of their domestic sanctuary. That architecturally romantic moment was literally jolted away when a shoulder tackle sent her flying to the ground, breaking her necklace and scattering beads and stones across the drive. The scream of a Blue Jay in mid-dive created accompanying sound effects. While making sure that all parts of her were where they were supposed to be, she had time to wonder *Who's scripting this? Am I part of a writers' conference? Or a reality T.V. show?*

"Sorry, ma'am." *Ma'am? My mother's "ma'am." Injury after injury,* she thought as she tried to pick herself up. *I'm just thirty.* She felt a nick of her conscience. *Well, I forgot about that last birthday. 31.*

Mary Beth half heard the trying-to-be-gentle masculine voice continue, ". . . but that Blue Jay was making a nose-dive for the top of your head. I didn't mean to knock you over, just wanted to push you out of the way," he said as he helped her up. "I didn't want the bird to draw blood. See, the babies she's protecting are over there."

A few feet away, a line of vulnerable little Jays was crossing the driveway. Their fierce maternal protector had no way of knowing that this territorial intruder was harmless. Mary Beth brushed herself off, glad that she had the sense not to wear her white jeans for traveling. As she glanced up at her rescuer, she forced her mouth into her good-sport smile, a useful smile that she had often been told lit up her face.

When she looked at her handsome tackler, she was glad she had used her thirty-but-still-flirty wiles (*or wile,* she edited). *What intense blue eyes. I might get something more than an article out of this week.* She could feel her face flushing at the thought and quickly looked down, glad to hide her expressive face with the bead-hunting excuse. The man, too, got down on his knees to join her in picking up rolling beads.

He modestly introduced himself as Hans, without mentioning any awards. But Mary Beth knew Hans Thale Bout's reputation. After all, he had just received PEN's Golden Pen Award for his distinguished service to literature. She had expected him to be much older. This attractive stranger crawling around, chasing after rolling beads couldn't be more than 45. Hans was having trouble picking up the broken bits of jewelry. He thought the beads looked more like interesting seeds. In fact, he handed her a few small pods and multi-colored stones by mistake.

"I'm sorry," he said, "really sorry. Really sorry. Indeed I am. I meant to gently push you away from that avian attacker, not knock you down. Are you o.k.? I must be stronger than I think I am," he added. "And you aren't quite as athletic as you look. No, that's not the right thing to say either, is it? I shouldn't be commenting on your body when we just met." *Have we met*? he asked himself. *Did she introduce herself or not*? He was too flustered to remember. She was obviously another participant in the Lakeville writing seminar, and he didn't want to start off the week with an enemy. He had enough of those. That radiant smile she had offered him a minute ago had faded; the strained expression that supplanted it must mean that he was just making things worse with his extended explanation. He wished he was wearing a hat (he'd have to make sure one of his characters in his next play did), so he could tip it and jauntily walk away, straight through that magnificent house and out the back door if this first meeting with one of his "classmates" was an omen of what was to come. But if he left, he wouldn't see that smile (or the girl attached to it) again. Without realizing it, he put his hand in his pocket and clicked together a few of the sinuously designed beads he had saved as a memento.

Hans, too, had avoided writers' conferences, even turning down a stint at Yaddo, the renowned writers' colony at Saratoga Springs. He had repeatedly refused offers to teach. He was much too shy or self-conscious or perhaps realistic to think he could stand up in front of a group of bored to eager students and tell them how to write. He remembered with irritation that his ex-wife had said to him, "Hans, my dear, that's why you need such a big car, to make up for your lack of other strengths."

He still thought she had meant in his public persona. A firm tenet of his faith continued to be that writing is a subject that could not be taught. Not by anyone. But when his letter from "Ohio Creates" arrived with its provocative questions, he felt the organizers were bypassing his famous authorial self and writing directly to his soul: "Is there something more for you as a writer than being on the best-seller list? Are rewards your only goal?" The questions the letter asked moved him as, not incidentally, did the accompanying offer of all expenses paid. Also, the thought wormed in, this was an acceptable excuse to get away from his agent, who was after him about an overdue first chapter draft. Thinking about her had disturbed him then and still did. *The idea of her implying that this dreadful writer's block is a fancy term for laziness.*

"Ohio Creates" would be a week-long, free vacation at an experimental workshop where all six well-known writers and the two sponsors would simultaneously create their own and edit each other's work. The organizers' idea to have each writer represent a different literary niche piqued Hans's imagination. Perhaps, he hated to admit, the group's variety would fill him again with that genuine charge of inspiration that had fueled him when he was the *enfant terrible* of the theater. Now at 47 (Mary Beth's estimate was close), when other writers were reaching their peak, he was drying up. *Yes, I'll go,* he decided. *At the least, I'll get an article out of it. And Marian will be there.*

Chapter Four

Sunday, continued

An article was also one of the benefits Sara and Clara were determined to reap from the conference. They would have some fun, too. As experienced literary workshoppers, they knew that the week in Lakeville would give them a chance to break out of the beneficent-lady roles they played at home; they planned to stir things up a little.

The two women really weren't named Sara and Clara. They didn't use the names professionally either. But they were so used to answering to those names that they had begun to think of themselves as Sara and Clara even though their legal names were Lucylle Lucas and Edith Munson. They often told each other how good "Lucas & Munson" looked on their book covers as their publisher gradually amplified the fonts used for their names to overshadow their titles. They were unaware of the otherwise well-known literary rule-of-thumb: the larger the author's name is on the cover, the poorer the novel. And if made aware, they wouldn't have cared. They were extremely successful.

They were referred to as Sara and Clara after the main characters in their long-running cozy series. They had created an amateur detective Sara who, with the help of her cat Clara, spent the first books of the series solving murder after murder in the imagined, small town of Smithville, Va. (Smithville, pop. 2,500, must be the murder capital of the world. Sara and Clara alone had solved eleven murders there in the past nine years).

Secretly proud of their Sara and Clara monikers, the two writers weren't sure how to register when they arrived on Sunday. They solved this difficult problem of immediate recognition vs. legal identity by writing out their full names with Sara and Clara in parenthesis next to the appropriate name. They needn't have worried. The other conference participants rarely talked about them as individuals, instead they were referred to collectively as "the girls." This was undoubtedly a commentary on the two 55-year-old women, who still giggled, and who favored denim skirts and cat-embroidered cardigan sweaters.

"Look at the registration book, Sara. 'Hans Thale Bout'. I know the organizers promised him, but I didn't really expect him to be here. We're in the big time."

"And just above him, there's a Mary Beth Goldberg?" Sara managed to narrow her eyes and her lips, "Who's she?"

"I looked her up when we got the invitations. She's not exactly a well-known writer like the rest of us." Clara straightened her rather bulky shoulders to emphasize her "well-known" status. "But maybe she is somebody in the academic world. Who knows what they read? And she has written at least one book on E.M. Forster that had top reviews. Whoever she is, she must be in her mid-40s, maybe older." This wouldn't be Clara's last error during the week.

Sara's lack of response stimulated Clara to explain. "Did you ever meet any woman named Mary Beth who was under 40? Mary Beth doesn't even make the fifty-most-popular names list for today, but in the 1940s and 50s, it was pretty popular. That's when an infusion of middle name add-ons like Mary Lou, Mary Jane, and Mary Beth put the old-fashioned, good girl, just plain Mary back on the list."

"You're such another, Clara. How *do* you recollect all of that odd information? And why? I need a drink just thinking about it."

"Hey, I name all of the characters in our books. Anyway, everybody has a photographic memory. Some people just seem to have run out of film," she chuckled.

"On a more important subject, Sara, we're in luck. It looks like cocktail hour is about to start, but who knows what they'll serve," Clara cautioned. "Let's go up to our room first. According to this diagram, we're in the Melville Room. Let's see. That would be the second room from the head of that rather grand stairwell. I've got a Macallan single malt in my bag. My experience tells me we should fortify ourselves first, then drink whatever 'Ohio Creates' has to offer. And, remember, Marian will be there."

Before reaching the staircase, Clara took a quick detour to the left, Sara to the right. On either side of the hallway, niches had been carved above the wainscoting.

"Could this be mahogany?" Clara asked. "I'll bet it is," she answered herself. "And the marbleized walls have to be the originals," she added.

She was drawn to the marble bust on a pedestal in the deeper niche. The large brass plate affixed beneath the bust announced it as the portrait of Mr. Charles A. Syberstone, whom Clara knew had been the original owner of Prince George House. However, it wasn't Mr. Syberstone, but rather the jauntily tilted Stetson he was most inappropriately wearing that had attracted her. Such lese majesty would have been unthinkable in Syberstone's day. "That irreverent Western romance guy must be here," she called out to Sara.

Sara was too occupied to respond. The shallower niche on the opposite side of the hallway had attracted her. It housed a large mirror. The elaborately framed reflecting glass had been placed there by a knowing decorator to balance Mr. Syberstone's heavy bust on the other side, and was gratefully used by Sara, who wouldn't dream of making an entrance unless her bangs were perfectly aligned.

With a writer's eye for detail and not wanting to appear overly vain, even to Clara, Sara was quick to point out that she had another reason for looking at the mirror: the hand-carved curlicues of intricately linked wood that made up its frame were repeated in the refectory table placed against the adjoining wall.

"The banisters, too," Clara added as they reached the stairs. When they huffed their way up to the top of this elegant, but slightly askew, central staircase, Clara put her bag down for a moment while she activated its wheels. She heaved a few deep breaths necessary after the stair-climbing and bag-carrying exertion, patted her stone-washed denim jumper and herself back into shape, and gasped, "I wish they had an elevator. Why don't I just take a sit in this first room, Sara, while we explore it? In fact, why don't we explore all of the bedrooms? We can get away with it. They'll all perceive us as harmless, middle-aged women. They won't suspect a thing. See, this one has the door open, almost."

"Look, it's the one in front, the one with the balcony you can see from outside," Sara said as she gently eased the door to a truly open position. "We can always say we thought it was our room if someone catches us. And whether someone's there or not, we can take a look at it and compare it with what they're giving us." Sara compressed her lips, "A balcony, no less."

"Believe me, I'll complain if it's a better room than ours," Clara said, blotting her perspiring forehead with a tissue as she wheeled her carry-on into the bedroom labeled, "#1, Longfellow."

"Of course I believe you. How many years have I known you? I've actually come to admire your bitching. You know," Sara added, "as a writer I should have figured out a feline equivalent for 'bitching' by now!" A pat on the arm and an indulgent smile made the potential insult into a shared joke.

Sara shrugged her shoulders and (*why not?*) followed Clara into the room. No one was there, so they could safely look around, though Clara did her exploring from the vantage point of the arm chair. "Either that staircase is unusually steep or my fitness regime needs a slight improvement," she explained as she took in the specifics of the Longfellow Room.

The room was small, obviously a single. The red, pink, and white design of the heavily flowered chintz curtains was repeated in the wallpaper of one wall and again in pillows thrown on the arm chair that Clara was resting in. Fortunately it was a solid green—but the foot stool wasn't. More large flowers. And someone had managed to paint a floral frieze above all of the doors (entrance, closet, bath, balcony) in the already too-small room. Even the balcony looked smaller from inside. It was more decorative than useful, Clara and Sara had decided. The one wrought-iron chair and table it held wouldn't even be a heat-fighting necessity. A promised amenity for each room, the large ceiling fan that had turned on automatically with the light switch, promised coolness and prompted a few fan-factoids from Clara.

"Our hosts said that all the rooms would have modern ceilings fans, so you know I would have to look them up, and guess what? Some authenticity actually clings to using them. Peter Diehl invented the electric ceiling fan in 1882 just about when Queen Anne-style became an architectural fashion and people who could built houses like this. Not that the style had very much to do with the actual 18th century Queen Anne." She was on a roll, but Sara put an end to it.

"Clara, stop. It's enough that this room is just too much."

Satisfied that their room would be better (and a few minutes later, they saw that it was), they left quietly, closing the door behind them.

Isn't it odd that a room doesn't give out signals? Anyone looking into the room the way Sara and Clara had, would have no way of knowing that this ordinary single room, overly chintzed up to welcome a guest, would be the scene of a terrible crime within the next 24 hours.

audrey lavin

Chapter Five

later Sunday

The afternoon's cocktail party had gone as scheduled. But it had different effects on different people. It made Mary Beth think of the fierce competition of camel wrestling. It made Hans think of ways to escape, and made Clara and Sara think of the mixing of beverages as well as of people.

Participants had been invited to stop by for a drink and an informal meeting with their peers between 3 and 5 p.m. on Sunday. The bar was set up in the library of the mansion, a library that again brought back thoughts of Turkey to Mary Beth. With its high ceiling, inlaid marble floors, and wall to wall shelves full of books, the room reminded Mary Beth of the ruins of Ephesus's famous two-storied Roman library, even though the mosaics at Ephesus had been more elaborate than the geometric patterns of the marble floors she stood on to meet and greet. *Maybe no one else would find the two places similar. After all, the shelves at Ephesus held space for 12,000 scrolls, not Mr. Syberstone's sets of leather-bound volumes.*

What Clara and Sara noticed was that the house Scotch was 21-year-old Balvenie. They exchanged a "wow" look.

Mary Beth nodded a greeting to Hans who was busy studying the spines of shelf after shelf of leather-bound volumes. She met Clara and Sara and, as had many before her, thought that Clara really did look like the cat in her mystery series. *Were those little whiskers?* Mary Beth tried not to stare.

Then Marian Rogers walked in. Conversation stopped. Marian wore her striking, deliberately white hair in short spikes that must have taken her major mirror time to jell into place. She was dressed in what was obviously a designer suit. Everyone else was Connecticut casual (LL Bean) or Eastern intellectual (black with perhaps an exotic scarf picked up in one of those obscure Guatemalan villages.) In such a group, Marian's body-skimming, mini-skirted pink tweed stood out as she meant it to. The pashmina shawl, oh-so-casually thrown over one shoulder, was an ostentatious exclamation point. In different ways, everyone's clothes were purposefully eloquent. Participants packed thoughtfully; personal packaging was as well planned as their book covers.

But Marian's outfit did more than stand out. It screamed out. Did it scream out contempt at every one else's attempts to look arty and literary? Except for Mary Beth, the other five authors present were just as rich and just as cosmopolitan as Marian was, but most of them were highly invested in the reverse snobbism of dressing-down. The further contrast between the sophisticated way Marian presented herself and her well-known writing style of innocence and simplicity in her children's books struck almost every writer there. Some knew from experience that "innocence" and "simplicity" were not accurate descriptives for Marian.

Hostility became rife in the room. Looks were exchanged. Arms were crossed over chests. Clenched fists were hidden in pockets. Even Sara compressed her lips. Marian's faux diffidence to this wave of enmity was apparent to all. She walked over to the cheese tray with practiced carelessness. Conversation resumed.

"That's who's getting the CHINTZ bedroom," Sara, who had studied the housing diagram, snickered to Clara.

Clara nodded her recognition that someone was not going to be happy with that bedroom's over-decoration. "That'll be a hoot," she said.

"A hoot-and-a-half," Sara amended.

A man who neither Sara nor Clara had noticed walked up to Marian and immediately started to speak to her and only to her. His stance and facial expression were more aggressive than one would expect to see in a social setting. Whatever he was saying, Marian responded by keeping a determined half-smile on her perfect Stila-glossed lips. The stranger didn't look at anyone else in the room, though at least four heads were turned in his direction.

"There's 'the odd couple' for you," said Clara to Sara. For once she was right.

The stranger was, well . . . weathered would be the word for it, while Marian was the most un-weathered person there. The four other women saw her (some with admiration, some with resentment) as the epitome of *Harper's Bazaar* chic. The man talking to her was dressed in worn black jeans and snake-skin boots, with huge turquoise stones in his studded belt and bolo fastener. What kind of chic would that be?

Sara voiced the answer, "Would you call that ersatz Texas cowboy?"

The newcomer was H. Buck Carter, author of *those* Western romances. Carter's western vision had been formed where he was born, on the West side of Chicago. It had taken a concentrated effort to transform himself and move his background out to where the real West begins. Now he assumed the dress and mannerisms of the creator of low-bodiced, low-slung gun belt thrillers. Towering over Marian and sturdily built, he looked as if he should complete his big-sky country look by wearing a lumber-jack shirt instead of the black cashmere jacket that had obviously been hand-fitted to his muscular frame. His rugged face made him look older than his 45 years, but was tailor-made for book jacket photos. His skin was creased from the sun and wind except for white eye wrinkles, which made him look like he smiled a lot. But he wasn't smiling now. He looked angry as he pressed close to Marian. Bodice ripping didn't seem so improbable.

Not accidentally, Sara and Clara could hear the end of their conversation. Buck Carter's admonition, "Money doesn't buy happiness, m'dear" and Marian's sharp rejoinder, "You don't know where to shop." Still in character, Buck loped over to the bar.

The girls followed him.

"I have a Western joke you can use in one of your cowboy books," Clara volunteered, erring again, this time in her judgment of Buck, of what he wanted to hear and from whom.

Buck added to his already substantial glass of bourbon.

"A cowboy came into town on Friday." Clara persisted. "He left on Monday afternoon after a week's work. How could that be?"

Buck's voice was as rough as his face. "It couldn't be that the hoss he rode into town on was named Friday, could it, ma'am?" He finished his bourbon and turned away from them to pour another.

Passing over their rejection (they'd been there before), Sara and Clara set their sights on Hans. *I can't stand even one of their tentative mewings*, he thought as he, too, deliberately moved away from them and from the cocktail party. That rather impolite move was a negation by Hans of all of the noise passing for communication in the room. The walls seemed to be expanding with competitive verbal resumes. In safe opposition, his little corner contracted while he continued to closely study book titles. *What had the former owners been thinking? The fourteen volume* (he counted again) *Thompson Illustrated Library edition of Dickens shelved next to the paperback Tolkein tetrology.* He reflected on the orderly disorder of the books and the architectural wonders of the house he would be living in for a week. The size alone was comforting. For a week he would be residing in a protective bulwark against what he increasingly perceived as a hostile world. *Prince George House. Of course. The Danish consort of Queen Anne. What a dandy of a Queen Anne style house. And what an abundance of architectural detail. I'll have fun exploring.*

Hans wasn't sure about his relationship with the other writers, but he knew he would get along with the house, that it would like him as much as he liked it.

He thought back an hour or so to his first meeting with Professor Mary Beth Goldberg. *Was it really so awkward? She's the only one in this group who looks at all promising. Very promising*, he self-corrected. *Actually, this week seems to hold much more potential now than it did seven days ago.* He snuck a furtive look around. *I wish I had a periscope. I'd like to study these people without having to talk with them.* But he turned to look at Mary Beth again. She was surprisingly attractive for a woman he'd heard referred to as "THAT Professor." He hadn't read her academic works, but he knew of her popular non-fiction. He'd even read her last book about her experience teaching American Studies to convicted murderers in the maximum security prison of Spain. The whole concept blew his mind. He had pictured the author who could handle such an assignment, though for the life of him, he couldn't picture the studious murderers. He had even nick-named her Mary Beast. When he read Mary Beth's book, Hans could visualize her perfectly as a big woman, tall and heavy, a commanding presence in the prison, wearing no-nonsense shirts and trousers, a perfect Mary Beast. *Nothing like Mary Beth.* The comparison made him grin.

She was standing alone by the door now. He was determined to casually walk up to her. As he approached, he made strong eye contact, but only muttered, "Great party." Writing fluently does not necessarily equate with speaking fluently. Unable to think of anything to add to his critical appraisal of the cocktail hour, Hans touched Mary Beth gently on the shoulder and walked out of the door leaving her to think, *This is his idea of a great party? Sometimes I miss Tony. He might have embarrassed me by throwing in all those obscure quotes, but he is trying to write "Bartlett's BETTER Quotations," and, at least, he would have talked. Hans spent all of his time practically hiding in a corner, reading or pretending to read book titles.*

But those penetrating eyes. What did that look mean?

And was it necessary to read each title twice? The words don't change. . . I'll see what's there.

audrey lavin

Chapter Six

Sunday evening

Not then. She'd have to look later. Nikki and Malcolm Haverford, the organizers of "Ohio Creates" were making their entrance. In practiced unison, they sauntered into the room. In practiced unison, they lightly clinked a melodic rhythm on their champagne glasses to command the group's attention.

The house was Nikki and Malcolm's playpen—in ways that the assembled guests had yet to realize. It was filled with toys that the guests had yet to see.

But at the moment, Mary Beth's attention was turned to the tapping of the glasses: "Real crystal," she murmured to Marian, who had moved next to her.

Nikki introduced herself. A former teen-model, she was the skinniest woman anyone there had ever seen, something they discussed and agreed upon the minute she left the room. Nikki had dropped out of high-school to start her career, and even with years of modeling behind her, was, with Mary Beth, one of the youngest women there. But it was getting a little late in life for her to continue to play the teen-aged model. At 32 Nikki's closet contained an up-dated version of her trade-mark wardrobe from fifteen years ago. She still wore her blond hair in pigtails, this afternoon tied in pink bows to match her pink and white checked shorts, while her peasant blouse was placed demurely off of just one shoulder. She had been born in 1974, the same year as her buddy and fellow teen-aged super-model Kate Moss. But in contrast to Kate's young seductress, Nikki had played the innocent child. And she had never gotten over it.

"As you know, at this point in time, I am not a writer," she unnecessarily explained. "But the six of you are. You are writers with great vocabularies like, like—whatever. I might add you are writers at the top of your careers" (some preening here). "I hope you have all introduced yourselves to each other. At the end of the day, one thing you should know is that in addition to being chosen for excellence" (more preening, accompanied by forgiveness for her constant use of trite phrases), "each individual was invited as a writer who represents a different gender, oops, genre. In case you haven't figured that out, I'm going to introduce each writer and genre in alphabetical order.

"Hans Thale Bout, as you know, has written many plays and won many awards." Hans, as if on cue, re-entered the room. "His awards range from the London Arts Best New Writer Award for *Love Your Parables* when he was just out of grad school to last year's New York Critics Award for *Pray at your Passions* and this year's absolutely crowning achievement the Pen Achievement Award– and to such a relatively young man.

"Then we have Lucylle Lucas and Edith Munson. With all due respect, ladies, you are better known to all as Sara and Clara, those extremely awesome collaborators who write cozy detective novels. Who could forget Lucas and Munson daring to leave murderous Smithville to give us *Sara and Clara Find Blood on the Riviera*? And which of you remain unafraid when they ventured South for *Sara and Clara Find the Mystery at Tara*?

"The only one of you who is not a full-time writer is Dr. Mary Beth Goldberg, our well-known author and professor from Midfield Campus College, cruelly referred to as McCollege." Mary Beth grimaced, *Like that dig was necessary!* "As her people would say, 'If you can't say something nice, say it in Yiddish' " *What?* This time Mary Beth wasn't the only person who grimaced.

Nikki was still talking. "But I do have something nice to say. In addition to her academic work, Dr. Mary Beth Goldberg has written two popular non-fiction, first-person adventure novels that even today no one would expect a pretty young lady to be writing." (Mary Beth blushed and immediately resented her blushing as much as she resented receiving another sexist introduction.) "Her two new works combine her love of teaching with her love of writing, almost creating a new genre. That's a hard word to have to keep saying. As you hopefully know, the books are *Angelito, My Favorite Spanish Murderer* and *Firecrackers*? *Mi Sombrero*: *Machine Guns over San Salvador*.

"And Marian Rogers is here. Our Newberry Award winner. Incidentally my husband has had the privilege of illustrating both of the award books." Malcolm tried to keep a neutral facial expression. The result was a look that came and went so fast that Mary Beth couldn't figure out if it was a leer or a sneer. She wasn't alone in wondering what that was all about.

"That's alphabetical?" Clara whispered to Sara. "No wonder she's the model and we're the writers."

Sara gave Clara a look. "There are plus-size models," she said defiantly. "Quaggy bodies like ours can be interesting."

And petite-sized minds in some authors, Clara muttered to herself.

Nikki continued, "With all due respect, Harrison Buck Carter ("Oh, that's who was talking to you, Marian," Mary Beth whispered) is perhaps the most well-known of all (some unhappy expressions here) as his Western romances continue to sell like the proverbial hot cakes. In fact, *The Hellion's Hotcakes* has been on the *New York Times* best seller list for seven weeks in a row now and looks like it will surpass his own record of being *numero uno* on THE list for nine weeks."

"Y'ars ago I changed my handle from 'Harrison' to 'Buck,' little gal" Buck interjected. "That helped my career, and it'll help your introduction if you do the same. But I've got to give you credit. You've got more spurs that jingle jangle than I'll ever have. You must have rings n' things going through every available body part—I'll bet every conceivable part, too." He punctuated his last words with an unpleasant smile.

Nikki dropped her notes. She looked to Malcolm for help. None was forthcoming. She picked the notes up and stammered on: "Mal, I mean, Malcolm and I want to offer uninterrupted time for work to you six creative writers, may I say geniuses, (*Yes!* each writer smiled inwardly).

We have provided excellent working conditions for you and expect a supportive environment from your colleagues."

"I hope she's not into social engineering," Mary Beth whispered to Marian, who had been standing next to her during all of the introductions.

Marian almost snickered back, "From the atmosphere that greeted me a few minutes ago, I doubt if I have to worry about any socialization, even if it's enforced."

"The atmosphere did turn a little cool," Mary Beth said, "but I think the library's real temperature is set pretty low for June."

"Here, take my shawl," Marian responded. "All of the vibes in this room are over-heating me."

Mary Beth gratefully wrapped herself in the lovely pashmina as she and Marian turned their attention back to Nikki and her introductions: "And finally, I'm happy to present *my* (Marian was not the only one aware that the possessive pronoun was stressed for her benefit) my Malcolm, who right now is having concurrent one-man shows in the contemporary art museums of Cleveland and Chicago." She continued to read from the notes that had obviously been written by Malcolm: "All critics agree that he finds the essence of his sitters through his original combination of high-tech photography and low-tech art installations.

"I'm going to take just one minute for some business before you hear Malcolm's creative ideas for this week. Don't worry," she added in response to some looks of apprehension that were appearing in her small audience. "It's not business requesting funds, more like mail call at camp. No surprises." (They would recall this remark later.) "Some of you have received packages and mail 'to be held for arrival.' "

Not unexpectedly, a box of candy and some flowers had arrived for Marian. Marian received her packages graciously, glanced at the cards, and went toward the kitchen to look for a vase. Everyone seemed to have a letter or a package.

"Mary Beth," Nikki called out. Mary Beth recognized the handwriting on the letter. And the address. Who else but Tony? She was glad that Nikki hadn't seemed to notice that it was addressed to "Dr.

Mary Babe Goldberg." She put the letter in the back pocket of her black dress-jeans to read later Sunday evening. *Was Tony beginning to realize that maybe a two-week's separation wasn't such a good idea, after all? Her-week-away plus his-week-away might be more than they needed to test their relationship.* Nikki was pushing a book-mailing envelope in her direction; she reached out for it.

A *package for me*? Mary Beth ripped off the plain Manila wrapper, noting the return address was the *Philadelphia Inquirer.* A memo fell out, 'Please review *Billy Blue* for a Young Readers book section.' *How odd,* thought Mary Beth when she saw the book. *They must have me mixed up with Marian. This is a picture book, definitely written for little children.* By then Marian was back in the room, placing her vase of flowers on the piano. "Marian, you take it," Mary Beth said. "I don't read this stuff. Even if I did, I don't know anything about kiddie lit crit."

"I'd love to," Marian replied crossing the room to Mary Beth and almost grabbing the book. "I don't know if the *Inquirer* will let you sub-contract an assignment, but I know that upstart author and I can't wait to let him have it."

"Thanks, Mare, uh, Marian. I'll e-mail the book editor. I'm sure he'll be thrilled to have someone with your reputation doing the review."

"End of mail-call," Nikki was announcing." During the rest of the week, you'll find your mail on the refectory table in the front hall. As soon as everyone quiets down, Malcolm will answer some of your questions by explaining the vision driving our mission."

Marian whispered back to Mary Beth, "That 'vision' has given him the reputation of an amiable monomaniac. I hope amiable is the key word there." Little did she know.

Malcolm plunged into his talk the same way he plunged into his art and his theories—without too much thought as to where he was going.

"The unity of all of the arts is my dream. Do not we all express our souls in our work? Do not all of our souls partake of the one great soul or, if you prefer, call it nature? Or the inspirational font? Or whatever you choose to call it. I, as a visual artist, draw from the springs of my inner being just as you literary artists do. And all of you who write in different genres are one under the skin."

Marian's and Mary Beth's eyes met; in an almost choreographed moment, they turned to the bar. Mary Beth was surprised at how much she liked Marian. Before she left Midfield Campus College (McCollege, as Nikki had pointed out), she had been prepped by her good friend Abby to dislike Marian on sight.

Marian whispered again. "I'd hate to think that my work is one under the skin with Sara and Clara's cozy mysteries. I can't stand them. Each formulaic story has that same damn cat and some recipes. Now, if they'd have a recipe that listed cat as one of the ingredients, that might be different."

Sara and Clara were standing fairly close. *Had they heard? Too bad.* Marian was not embarrassed.

Mary Beth smothered her laughter at Marian's joke. Even a grin right now would be exceedingly inappropriate as Malcolm, also inappropriately, was now in the middle of quoting George Eliot: "'It has begun already—the marriage of our souls.' Our drawing together here to create, to meditate will melt soul into soul, one art into another, making all thought fuller 'as the clear waters are made fuller, where the fullness is inseparable and the clearness is inseparable.' "

The other four writers became inseparable with Mary Beth and Marian at the bar. No one mentioned THE speech, which seemed to be over. But much eye-rolling and eyebrow-raising accompanied the simplest requests for ice or glasses.

Nikki was tapping her glass for attention again.

"We'll go right in to dinner tonight as this inspirational cocktail hour has gone on longer than we expected. But I hope you've enjoyed the chance to schmooze," she announced with a smile directed at Mary Beth.

"For the rest of the week, cocktails will be served from five to seven. Dinner at seven will be the only meal Malcolm and I expect all of you to attend. That is, dinner each evening and tomorrow morning's breakfast, which will be from seven until nine. After that, breakfast and lunch will be optional. You can join us in the dining room for buffet meals or, if you don't want to interrupt your work, you can have a tray or box lunch delivered to your room. Please let Cook know the night before if you want delivery to your room. Please let me know 24/7 if there is anything Malcolm and I can do to make the conditions here more optimum for your work. And now, *bon appetit*."

Nikki's 'more optimum' added too much icing to Malcolm's philosophical cake for Sara and Clara. They weren't the only writers who reacted to the phrase. It was the straw that broke the camel's back for Mary Beth, "get me out of here" for Hans, and "Oh my, her roots *are* showing (educational, not cosmetic)" from Marian. With Malcolm's lecture on personal theory in mind, a somewhat subdued group filed into the ornate dining room as if it were their last meal. For one it was.

audrey lavin

Chapter Seven

Monday morning

The discovery of Marian's body on Monday morning brought a decided atmospheric change. Architecture, Turkish memories, one-upmanship, and even romance took back seats while all waited for the ambulance.

Cook was starting to clear the table of the morning's congealed left-overs when the Basic Life Support unit arrived. "Twelve minutes," Sara announced, eyes on her watch. She had temporarily turned a catastrophe into a research project, timing emergency response for the next Sara and Clara cozy.

Mary Beth, Hans, and Sara were awkward in the face of death. But the professionals were not. As the two-man crew entered the room, they pulled on latex gloves. "Has anyone administered CPR?" the E.M.T. asked as he bent over the victim and started the procedure. No one had; they'd been unwilling to touch the too-perfect, stone-still body.

"No results," the para-medic announced. It had taken the two men only a few minutes to ascertain death. "Does anyone know the woman's medical history?"

"No one knows. Her theory was 'Don't complain. Don't explain,' " Hans said.

Malcolm, who had just joined the upstairs group, corrected him. "She told me, 'Don't excuse and for Pete's sake, don't recuse.' "

The citation fight that would follow Marian through national obituaries was just beginning.

Sara kept pleading, "No results? Are you sure? Are you sure?" The well-muscled E.M.T. gently explained to her that the team could find no evidence of respiratory or cardiac activity in the body, which meant that "death" was the only diagnosis. Mary Beth noticed that Sara managed to overcome her shock by placing her hand on the arm of the young E.M.T. She tried to start a conversation with him, in a tone as roguish as a woman in her mid-fifties, supposedly in mourning, could, "And are you going to medical school?"

"No," the young man politely, but emphatically, replied, "I like to be outside —and free."

Sara writes murder mysteries; maybe unexplained, unexpected death stimulates her, thought Mary Beth.

The driver waited outside while the emergency team carefully shooed the concerned writers out of the Longfellow room and put a "Crime Scene" tape across the door.

"I thought it was a heart attack. What crime are you guys talking about?" demanded Hans, who had appointed himself group spokesman.

Eric, the young E.M.T., addressed the four writers, "We're not saying a crime has been committed here. But we are required by law to treat a dead body as part of a crime scene and to insist on minimal traffic. Look, you all can understand that if, for example, the police later find out that this woman was murdered and we've let everyone march in and out of her room—this is her room, right? Well, we would have really messed up the crime scene. Or if we passed around some of the chocolates on her desk and they turned out to be a clue . . . On the other hand, if it's just a heart attack (*JUST a heart attack?* Mary Beth wondered) no harm done in keeping people out."

This was not the "sanctuary for writers and writing" that had been promised in the invitation to "Ohio Creates." At least not for Marian.

Eric's explanation was interrupted by the arrival of three police officers: two men and Officer Lois. They didn't have to badge their way in. This was Ohio, polite and accepting of authority.

The B.L.S. group had done its job and prepared to leave. They first told the police that they were noting in their run report the almost too-perfect position Marian had been found in. The precise centering of her head on the pillow could be satisfying an unknown someone's need for order and balance.

Malcolm, who'd come upstairs with the two E.M.Ts, intervened, "That effortless, photo op perfection of hair and make-up is not unusual if you know Marian."

The policeman in charge ignored Malcolm's attempt to play the role of alpha male and nodded agreement to Eric as the E.M.T. team members picked up their gear and left the now over-crowded room. They were accompanied down the steps with fervent thank you's and more than a bit of leaning on young Eric by Sara. Managing to keep their dignity, the men waited in the entrance hall for further orders.

Upstairs, Hans had moved to Mary Beth's side. He held her eyes for a couple of beats. Then noticing that her face was still blotchy red with emotion, he let her have the personal space she needed. Lois, the only woman in Lakeville's police department, consoled them. This was her job, the job she was always given and always resented. But with enforced practice, Lois was now at the point where she did it very well.

Lois was also the official photographer. She took out her camera, brushed back her frizzy red hair, and photographed all aspects of the room and body, making sure she had a close-up of Marian's strange smile. After she had taken her pictures, and the chief had asked a few questions, she called for the E.M.T. team to come back to the room to remove the corpse. It took the two men only a few minutes to place Marian, or Marian's body, on a gurney and take her down to the waiting van. It was some compensation to Lois that the department's sharp division between men's work and women's work meant that she didn't have to handle the corpse.

The police were particularly sensitive to what they perceived as the potential for lawsuits from the nationally-known author-types now inhabiting Prince George House. They didn't need any bad publicity either. And they knew that the *Lakeville Ledger's* official car, carrying its official crime reporter, would be parked outside by the time they left. So they returned to Marian's room only to bag a few items: the box of candy on the desk, the book she had been reading, her recently worn clothes, and her computer. Lois stayed a few minutes longer. She felt that guestrooms had a remarkable way of assuming the personality of their inhabitants. She wanted to absorb as much as she could. If this was not a natural death, she would be put in charge of the investigation. She allowed herself a moment of pride in her recent promotion to detective. She decided she would immediately order a general finger printing of household inhabitants, just in case.

When she was ready to leave, the police stretched and added to the yellow crime scene tape already on the door so that it would go around the room and announced, "A precaution to preserve the scene. Entrance to this room is restricted to authorized investigators." This was not the reassurance that the concerned writers who were still upstairs needed.

The chief first made his announcement upstairs in the hall between the Longfellow and the Melville rooms. He repeated his words downstairs where the remaining guests and their hosts were gathered, "All right, people, you know what the tape means. Respect it. One deputy will remain to see that you do. He reports any infringements directly to me. We'll be back later."

Malcolm, as host ('prime mover' was the way he saw his role) said he would notify Marian's family. "Actually I don't know her family, but I do know her agent. I'll phone her up and let her handle all of the disturbing details." Malcolm was also the first to say he would miss Marian.

"I loved her style and flamboyance," Malcolm announced to the authors milling round in the library. "In such flamboyance I found the poetry that counteracted her childish kiddie lit. Seeing her in bed like that was seeing a black and white photograph of the technicolor Marian I knew." Hans walked in, ready to object. But it was Buck who cut Malcolm off, "Enough of your personal history. I'm the trail boss here, podner." He couldn't keep it up. His braggadocio and even his cowboy couture seemed to have lost some of their flair.

Still, Hans muttered to Sara, "He's so far gone into that cowpoke role he's playing, you wonder how he'll ever come back."

Buck startled them both with a physical turn as well as an appropriate mental one, "Was that the kiddie lit book you gave her to review, Mary Beth, the book she was reading when she died?"

Mary Beth shook her head, "No, I could see by the size that it wasn't. It looked like one of the bindings from the library here. I can picture that book. I can see and smell the whole scene all over again."

Sara leaned over to Clara, "That's pretty good. All I noticed was that she wasn't reading one of our books."

Mary Beth's voice became more intense. She began to tremble in a delayed reaction. "It's all my fault. I should have checked on her sooner. Maybe if I'd come up to the room earlier, this wouldn't have happened."

Sara didn't say anything, but helped Mary Beth gain control by gently taking her hand. "How long has Marian been dead? Does anyone know," she asked.

"Detective Lois said she died some time during the night." Hans said.

"You don't have to be a detective to figure that one out," Sara cut in. "We saw her last night at dinner and didn't see her at breakfast, so yes, I'd guess it was during the night."

"Lois did say a little more. She said that she would give a more exact time later and that she'd be able to figure it from Marian's body temperature. Lois said that the body cools at three degrees an hour at first. By the time Marian was found, her body was cooling at one degree or less. I'd say less; she was cold."

"What are you talking about? Bodies. Temperatures. I can't believe any of it," Mary Beth said. "It was only yesterday, more like twelve hours ago, that Marian and I were laughing together." She caught herself before she said that they had been laughing at Sara and Clara's writing and at Malcolm's pontificating. "We were talking in the library, maybe on the way to being friends, and now she's dead. It doesn't seem possible." Then she remembered how Malcolm, Buck, and Hans had changed expression, presumably thinking of their past relationships with Marian. Had any one of them been thinking of a future rendezvous with her? No one would have it now,

"With all the mysteries I've written, we've written," Sara corrected herself after a look from Clara, "outside of a funeral, I've never seen a dead body before. It was horrible. The horror." She started to cry.

Hans thought, *the real horror is that there is no horror here.*

Buck squeezed Sara's hand in a surprising (to Mary Beth) show of warmth and turned to the assembled group, "Look, Marian's not coming back. Go out for a walk. Git along, little . . . " He self-corrected his Western persona again, "My bad. Cry. Go back to your writing. Work this out the best you can." Even this small indication that Buck understood his Westernisms would now be inappropriate surprised some of his audience.

It made Mary Beth slightly shift her original opinion (*All bluff. All surface.*) of him. She was to keep her original opinion of Malcolm (Lost in the perilous construction of a personal critical theory).

"Yes. Yes," Malcolm was adding to Buck's message, "Go to the gardens. See for yourselves where I find the elements for my paintings and photography that relate to my Arcadian renaissance. The land this house sets on is believed to be the source of mystical creative powers. Go barefoot. Let the power enter. Let it straighten your auras. It can cure us of our sorrow, our loss."

"Cure us?" Mary Beth thought of Tony and his idea of a cure (Acupuncture is a jab well done.) She missed him. She missed his fun in bed. *What would that new guy Hans be like in bed?* she allowed herself to wonder. *What is the matter with me? The older I get, the trampier I get.* Then she felt a twinge of genuine guilt. *Marian would never miss any of her boyfriends again.*

Clara and Sara, who were on the couch comforting each other, had a different response. They decided to partake of the mystic curative and creative powers of the bottle of Macallan they still had in their room.

With Clara curled up in the arm chair and Sara sitting on the bed, the two friends raised their water tumblers and sipped the scotch. Reinforced, "the girls" talked over the rather startling events of the morning.

"I'm glad I'm not one of those no-alcohol-before lunch people. Aren't you, Sara?"

"Um-hmm. Poor Marian." Sara pursed her lips, "Do you think that was really a heart attack? How could it be? Not a spike in her hair was out of place. Can you will yourself to die neatly?"

"She wasn't 'neat.' I'd say it was a pretty glamorous pose. Can you will that?

"I can't believe she planned it. She didn't seem like the suicidal type to me. We can ask the guys who know–knew—her. But it doesn't have to be a heart attack. Maybe it was an aneurism."

Sara stopped her medical guessing game and made a suggestion: "Let's snoop around a bit. We don't have to wait for the medical report. We have plenty of experience."

"Yoo hoo, Sara. That experience is all fictional. And we don't have a cat to help us this time," Clara said with a half-smile.

"Come on, Clara, let's go for it."

audrey lavin

Chapter Eight

Monday afternoon

Downstairs in the library, a similar conversation was going on. The initial shock at the discovery of Marian's too-perfectly arranged body had worn off; suspicions were beginning to build. Lunch had been light, eating it, almost furtive. Mary Beth had carried her cup of green tea and chocolate chip cookies (good health and good energy sprang from separate sources) to the library, where she mulled over the possibility of writing a piece (*creative non-fiction?)* about Marian's death. She was experienced in on-the-spot, you-are-there-now adventure writing, but she had never written about a situation that was expanding to include the possibility of murder.

She turned to Hans who had joined her on the library couch. He hadn't said much since they had left Marian's room, but Mary Beth felt somehow that even his silence was supportive. She was grateful. "Hans, do you think it indecent if I take some notes and write this up? We don't know that it's a murder; it could easily be a natural death, but either way, Marian is a well-known writer, a public figure in her world. You know I have a lot of experience in interviewing for my academic adventure books. I'll bet I could gather a bundle of information, especially if I start right now, before people have their guards up. I'm sure I could get a long article, most probably a book out of it. I think I should write a quick synopsis and register the idea. What do you think?"

Hans answered the way she hoped he would: He reached out with an affirming touch. "We discovered the body together. Let's work together. I'll follow your investigation wherever it takes us, and I'm not going to try to write a book about it. I'm not saying that I might not incorporate some details in my next play, but this can be your story. And an intriguing journey for your readers. Didn't you help solve a crime a year or two ago at Midfield? You and your boyfriend?"

Hans was quiet.

Mary Beth was quiet.

After that few second conversational delay that seemed like a few hours, Mary Beth said proudly, "Yes, with my boyfriend, Tony, the engineer and editor." She thought back; she thought ahead, and added, "He's not exactly my boyfriend now."

Hans moved closer, "That's good enough. I'm in this with you, Mary Beth." For the briefest second longer than what is socially acceptable, he held her eyes with his. They both immediately looked out of the window. Was there something fascinating about seeing cardinals in Ohio?

Slightly self-conscious without knowing why, Mary Beth tried to move the subject to a less personal arena, but it was impossible to keep away from what had occurred. She moved herself instead of the subject and walked into the adjoining parlor. Hans followed. "Are we supposed to have a funeral? She must have family. What about a memorial service?"

Mary Beth's stomach shifted a little. *Marian had been so alive only yesterday. I still have her pashmina shawl.* Then the implications of Hans's suggestion hit her, "I hate to be disrespectful, but if the service is here, there's no way we're going to keep Malcolm from eulogizing."

Hans nodded. "He'll ask us each to write a spontaneous tribute, no revisions."

"That's not writing; that's typing!" Somewhere along the line Buck had wandered into the parlor and joined the conversation. "Speaking of writing, I'm sure I've thought of this first: I'm going to be the one to do a little creative interpretation of Marian's death. I'm registering the idea today."

Mary Beth's jaw dropped. She exchanged looks with Hans. Before they could compete with Buck, he continued: "Before The Girls went back upstairs, they tried to tell me they were writing this up. They even had a title that they wanted to register. It's the world's clumsiest and, as far as I know, completely untrue, except that Marian is, I mean, was, a rare bird: *Sara and Clara/Solve The Murder Avis Rara.* I've seen to it that they've changed their minds."

Mary Beth's jaw dropped again. She had thought jaw dropping was something that just happened to characters in books until she felt her own mouth open wide. She looked at Hans again. His face and jaw were a mirror of her own. *Would the camels never stop shoving?*

She tried to bring the subject back to Marian and the possibility of a memorial service. "Instead of Malcolm's taking over, I know something that would marginally involve him and would be a lovely tribute. I don't know why the custom has been lost, but two years ago when I was in Izmir, Turkey, where the lost beads were from . . . Don't worry; I know you were trying to help me."

Hans's fingers automatically caressed the few beads he had saved in his pocket as a talisman.

Mary Beth was explaining, "Remember that Izmir conference I told you about? Before it started, I played tourist and went to see an archeological dig right in the city. It was in the old Agora, the ancient Roman city's market. When I first looked at it, all I saw was a big, dusty space surrounded by old pillars and foundations. But when I looked more closely, I could see that the stones marking the ancient graveyard were still there in the ruins. Each tombstone was topped with the hat showing the dead person's profession."

"You mean like a toque for a baker. Or a Stetson for me?"

"Well, I didn't see any ancient toques or Stetsons, but I did see different army helmets, some royal crowns. and tradesmen's hats.Wouldn't it be great to put a pen and ink . . . "

"No, no, Mary Beth, you always see that quill pen and ink pot with pictures of Shakespeare. Today it would be a computer. Now tell me, do you want a computer on your gravestone? Where's the romance in that?"

Mary Beth could feel herself blushing at Hans' use of the word 'romance.' *I've got to stop this,* she thought. *Now is not the time to publicly display a woman's crisis of self-confidence when talking to an attractive man.* She forced herself to speak. "We'll think of something. We could keep Malcolm busy making a small monument for the grave and ask him to make the magnanimous gesture of presenting it to the family. If they want to use it, fine. If not, fine, too. It will serve its main purpose of keeping our self-designated speaker-in-residence from delivering a week-long peroration."

Buck interrupted, "You might not have to worry your purty little heads about a service."

"Why's that?" Hans challenged.

"Marian had it all planned. You know that gal was controlled (Mary Beth thought of that perfect hair style) and controlling (Hans thought of all of the relationships he *knew* about). And I'll bet the posse, Hans, that you know she never could tell a joke. She was too literal and too authoritative. It really got to her that every time she started to tell a joke, people would actually walk away. So she planned that at her funeral, the minister would read a couple of her jokes and no one could decently leave! Still controlling from the grave."

Mary Beth thought out loud, "She'd have the last laugh, after all?"

Buck added, "Speaking of Malcolm's work, I'm an artist, too.

"Yep, before I rode the rodeo circuit, I had quite a little reputation in the Big Sky Country for my wood carving and paintings. I had a number of one-man shows." He hitched up his non-existent gun belt again.

"You were in the rodeo?"

"You're an artist?"

Buck answered looking at Mary Beth, "You come out to the lonesome prairie with me, little gal, and I'll show you there's nothing I cain't do."

Chapter Nine

Tuesday

Tuesday was a working day, a day of seclusion, perhaps of mourning. Seeking refuge in their work, most writers had meals delivered to their rooms. No group activity brought all of them together during the day.

Buck loved being in The Hemingway Suite. It was fitting, he thought, as he attacked his newest novel with a style that was forceful on many levels. He didn't stand, but rather sat down in front of his computer and literally began pounding the keys. "The lusty, busty hustler," he wrote and stopped. *Hell, I might as well make her Rusty, too—all over*, he grinned and went back to his pounding. "Hostess or hustler, Rusty knew what she liked. She liked men. And they liked her. Thinking about them, she moaned with pleasure and licked her lips. Like many good entrepreneurs, she had decided to make a business out of her hobby."

Across the hall, Sara and Clara had developed a system for co-writing novels that depended on conversation and legal pads. "Let's start right out in chapter one with breakfast," Sara suggested. "We've never used our great granola recipe."

"Great and more than slightly fattening," her co-writer said, patting her stomach.

"How about if we start this way, 'Little did Sara the sleuth know when she fixed her favorite granola recipe for breakfast (recipe p. 17 or wherever chapter ends) and fed Clara her favorite kitty granola (recipe p. 18 or wherever) that this would be the last peaceful breakfast the middle-aged detective and her cat would be having for some time?' "

"That's just fine. Add the word 'attractive' to middle-aged detective and let's have a body left on the front porch. She could trip over it when she lets the cat out."

At the same time, Hans was sitting in front of his computer. He went to "Office" and to "New Document." He sat facing the blank page. *The damn computer is my friend, not my enemy.* He got up and walked around the room. *It's my new agent who's my enemy. No matter what she says, I do not have 'literary inertia.' What a stupid phrase. I'm goal oriented. I know how to work through pain. I was a boy genius. I'm a talented writer. Maybe I need some inspiration.* His mind drifted off to Mary Beth.

She was across the hall, writing in her pedantic academic mode. "Brit v. Yank" she typed. *No, that's not specific enough.* She changed her title to "E. M. Forster's Put-Down of Henry James," and continued with "If Edward Morgan Forster meant his first published novel *Where Angels Fear to Tread,* 1905, to be read in part as his response to Henry James's *The Ambassadors*, 1903, no one noted it at the time of publication. In fact, if he planned *Angels* as a subtle correction to James's over-dependence on pattern that he was to criticize later in his *Common Place Book* and *Aspects of the Novel*, he succeeded very well." Mary Beth stopped. *Is that sentence too long? Should I unpack it?*

Yet with all of this retreat into the business of creativity, somehow the suspicion that Marian had been murdered permeated the air. The rumor was an indoor mist that crept in through the cracks under the doors, inhaled and absorbed by each person.

At the cocktail hour, when writers emerged from the safe cocoon of their rooms or their studios, the preferred nomenclature, the unspoken thought came out in the open. It was discussed by all. When they gathered near the bar in the library, Nikki seemed to confirm the rumor.

As a permanent resident of Lakeville, she was a clinging, juicy tendril of the local grapevine. In a typical small-town cross- fertilization of relationships, her hairdresser, Jon André, was the current boyfriend of Lois, the policewoman. Mr. Jon, as he insisted on being called, had a sister also named Lois. The two Loises had met through the Lakeville chapter of the International Lois Club. The club's benefits were readily apparent in sister Lois's critical introduction of the new Lois to Jon André.

Clara also had a sister named Lois and had watched with amazement as those Lois clubs had sprung up all over the world. "Membership isn't exactly restricted," she had explained to Sara. "You just have to own up to being named Lois! It sounds like wherever there are two Loises, one of them starts a club."

"At last count," Clara, who loved to collect odd facts, informed anyone who would listen, "the U.S. had 55 clubs with over 4,000 Loises, and Canada had 24 with over 2,200 Loises."

Policewoman Lois had told her fellow-Lois (*or should it be sister-Lois,* wondered Mary Beth), and that Lois told her brother Jon André, who then told Nikki that it sure looked like murder to the police. Nikki started to quote Lois, slurring her words to fit what she considered Lois's Ohio-Appalachian accent. "The po-lice department was waitin' on the results of the blood test. But it sure looked like the whole testin' department was sleepin' in on Tuesday mornin'." Nikki concluded by saying that Lois hoped to see the report by Wednesday. "At this point in time, we all do," she added. "I told Lois to call tomorrow as soon as she *warshes* up." Nikki, who suffered from justifiably low self-esteem, heard the response of silence as a condemnation. She knew she could change that judgment if she explained.

So she did: "That's my shtick," she said to Mary Beth. "I recognize different types. At least you're not kvetching."

Mary Beth had an escape: the bar was open. She decided that her usual pinot noir was too complicated for such a night and settled for a large glass of the earthier cabernet. *I'm astonished she didn't put out a bottle of Manischevitz, for me,* she thought. Sara and Clara had a simple agenda; they headed straight for the Balvenie. Buck and Hans each took a cold bottle of the only beer on the counter, Fischer's La Belle d'Alsace. "If I had a six-shooter, I'd use it if you ever tell any one I'm drinking this effete French stuff," Buck growled. Nikki had her nightly champagne cocktail. Malcolm, trying to keep a cool head, abstained. While in the kitchen, Cook and staff wrestled mightily with their problem: Was Jim

Beam the best bourbon to use to marinate the pork roast for tomorrow's dinner?

Even with the aid of that heavily used cocktail hour, dinner was a rather somber affair. Each writer left the dining room as early as he or she gracefully could. But once back in individual studios, each played over the events of the day. Nikki and Malcolm had the most to say to each other. Between opening their files for the sheriff and running the conference in the midst of a tragedy, they hadn't had much of a chance to speak privately since the discovery of Marian's body. When they entered their suite, they usually went directly to their work chairs at the cropping table. Tonight they sat side by side on their small couch with brandy snifters in hand.

"Before last night, I thought the worst conference we ever attended was the one in Bellevue. Remember? Even the motel was a downer."

"Do I remember? The lure of the promised Jacuzzi. What they didn't mention was that it wasn't even in the bathroom, but was right in the middle of the bedroom. The heart-shaped bed was another bonus. And that big mirror over it," Nikki laughed. "To be honest with you, I think tacky can be fun. And that was."

"Yes, but that was one of my first conferences. I still can't believe I packed the paper I was going to give on the 'Influence of Faux-Classical Mythology on My Contemporary Paintings.' "

"Well, you learned something, didn't you, when the airline lost your luggage and you had to sit at that panel table with a faux-classical goofy smile on your face and not say anything?"

"Now my new work will prove the obverse. It speaks for me. It is a demonstrable verification of my theories. Critics will see that my contemporary paintings and photography put a whole new face to faux-classical mythology, a new, un-rehearsed digital face to be exact." He actually smirked . Then came back to reality. "But Nikki this is really bad. The worst. Everyone, including the police, is saying that Marian was murdered."

"Do you think you ought to show detective Lois your photographs?"

"No, I don't."

"And they're not photographs," Malcolm corrected. "They're videos."

"I hear what you're saying, oh, camcorder king. But bear with me for a minute, sweets. They're all of people arriving, right? And Marian wasn't murdered, if she was murdered, when she arrived. So at the end of the day, what's the point in time? I mean, the point. What's the point?"

"What's your point, Nikki?"

"You know what, my dear, you're more in Never Never Land than usual. I think you and I need a good night's sleep. And don't worry about any moral implications of my film. Remember if electricity comes from electrons, then morality comes from . . . "

In his room Hans was thinking of Mary Beth while trying to send a document to his literary agent. *She's sexy, especially for an academic,* he thought. *She's smart. And I like punctual. But is punctual necessarily a valued good? Or does it just mean that she has nothing better to do than to show up*? He gave up on both counts. He decided he'd think about Mary Beth and send the document tomorrow.

His present goal: coaxing his recalcitrant computer to action. Unable to reach the emergency number for Ernie, the local computer geek who had installed the PCs for "Ohio Creates," Hans decided to try an online technician. He felt it would just take a few minutes for a tech to walk him through getting rid of the primary colored tracking marks that were now showing up all over his document. Those telltale tracking colors and symbols showed every addition and deletion and would tell the agent more than Hans wanted her to know. All of those corrections didn't look like someone with Hans's reputation of always having a sure knowledge of the precise word to use.

Words appearing on the screen drew his attention to them.

Welcome <boutman@aol>. Welcome to your computer's Live Help Area. A Customer Care Consultant will be with you shortly. His name is Sean.

Hans says, Welcome on board, Sean.

Sean says, Which board?

Hans hopes Sean is being humorous and decides to go right to his problem: When I copy and paste part of a document to email, all trackings are shown. How can I stop this? The tracking does not show up on original document, just on the email copy.

Tech Sean says, I appreciate the opportunity to handle this for you, Hans, with live technical support :=)

Hans says to himself :=) *What is this? An emoticon? Am I talking with a kid or a professional?*

Tech continues, You are referring to blue line on the vertical, right?

Hans says, No. I am referring to all changes made in a document I've written. The red, the blue, the green, the tracking for every word added or deleted shows up. None of this shows up in original document. Only when I email.

Tech says, Hans, when you copy and paste, it will only paste the message you have selected and pasted (Hans yanks his hair). No other extra words added and no missing words. Make sure you have highlighted the exact words or message you wish to copy and paste.

Hans types detailed message of how he copies and pastes, and points out again: When the document prints on email, it is not the same thing I copied and pasted originally. It shows every change I've made. That's what tracking is, but I don't want that information (in living color) to go to my literary agent.

Sean types, That would only happen if you got the message from a different source such as from a website or from another document. However if it is just copied from the same document, there would be no changes then.

Hans gnashes his teeth. I agree that there should be no changes. But there are changes on all 75 pages.

Tech Sean says, Since they are not came from same source or same window, that is the possible things to happen that there is a changes. And you just need to edit or arranges it then.

Hans thinks, *I've got this guy rattled. I'll make nice.* Where are you located?

Tech says, Other country. It is outside U.S.

Hans thinks, *No kidding*!

Tech types, You can change or arranges it from Write Mail window. It is like you are arranging the compose email.

Talking to himself again, Hans says, *I've got to be careful. This guy is turning into a basket case. Remember, so was Moses.* Trying to be nice, he patiently types, Where outside the U.S.?

Tech, I'm sorry I did not say need to rewrite it. It is already there and you just need to arrange it and not rewrite it. And adds, I am from the Philippines.

Hans says, This would be hundreds of corrections. Do you understand?

Tech says, Copying the message may cause the problems.

Hans says, Yes. Yes. That's what I've been saying. Copying the message DOES cause the problem. What I want to know is if there is any way I can correct the problems.

Silence. No copy received.

Hans types. I take it that you can not help me. He signs off.

I wonder if <GetHuman.com/us/> could help. Something else to think about tomorrow. I'll add it to my list.

audrey lavin

Chapter Ten

Wednesday

Awaking early Wednesday morning, Sara and Clara were determined to track down the E.M.T. squad and follow clues. How much Sara wanted to solve the crime and how much she wanted to track down Eric remained to be seen. For the occasion she carefully selected her best Land's End denim dress, the one with little kittens embroidered on the pockets. Though usually ostentatiously natural-looking, Sara added just a brush of blusher and light eye shadow (to help her detective work?). As a final touch she pulled on heavy blue socks and with more effort than she cared to admit, bent over to strap on her Trevas. Patting her hair back into place, she turned to Clara, "Do you think I'll pass muster?"

"If you don't pass muster, you can always pass the Macallan."

Mean thought Sara, but said only, "Clara, how do we find Eric and the rest of the squad?"

"We'll call a cab and ask the driver. This is a small town. He'll know. Anyway, I'm guessing that the rescue station must be located in the nearest fire station. That's where it was in our one attempt at science fiction, *Sara and Clara in the Wrong Era*. Do you recollect?" She laughed.

When the taxi arrived, Gary, the slightly balding, cigar-smoking driver, confirmed Clara's guess. But he wasn't in as much of a hurry as Clara and Sara were. He took the meandering way to the fire station so he could spend more time with "the girls." Eager to hear their versions of the mysterious events in the Syberstone mansion, he wasn't shy about showing off his own knowledge either. This was an opportunity not to be wasted: "It's not the first time there's been a murder there, y'know?"

Their incredulous, "No?" was all the fuel he needed to continue his story.

"When the house was built back in the 90s, that's the *1890s*, old Mr. Syberstone shot the architect, right in the library room." He started to laugh, anticipating his own joke: "He really shot him in the heart, but they were in the library!"

"But, why?"

"It was *old* Mr. Syberstone, but beautiful, *young* Mrs. Syberstone, and she and the architect were canoodling together. Lakeville legend tells it that the architect even built a hidden staircase from somewhere on the ground floor to her room so he could canoodle more conveniently. He sealed up the staircase, never told anyone where it was. And they called the murder a Crime of Love? Was it a Crime of Fashion? No, a Crime of Passion, so Syberstone got off Scott-free."

The cab driver entertained them with more small-town gossip. Sara and Clara, not the coolest cats around, were smart enough to know that most of what they were hearing was manufactured fable, but as story tellers themselves, they enjoyed listening to the tales and to the rhythm of his words. He was already calling theirs, "The Monday Morning Murder," even though it happened on Sunday night, and, as Clara reminded Sara later, "It might not be a murder; it could still be that heart attack 'Dr.' Mary Beth diagnosed."

"A poet of the people," Sara commented as they entered the fire station. She looked at the card the driver had pressed on them as they got out of the cab, 'Gary from Indiana.' She laughed. "And a natural punster, too."

"What about the Syberstone killing? Do you think that was true?"

"What about his saying that Marian was killed on Monday morning when we all know it was Sunday night? It's conceivable that a germ of truth is behind the alliteration, but I wouldn't believe any of his entertaining tip-enhancers. Let's just say he has a great sense of rumor."

At that minute, Sara started to turn bright red, out of character and out of context with anything Clara was saying. Clara turned to look for the reason. No surprise.

"Hey, Eric."

"Hey, Ms. . . . I'm sorry I've just come in from another run. I'm beat. It was terrible. Terrible. And I've forgotten your names."

"Oh, just call us Clara . . ."

"And," interrupted her friend with what she didn't realize was a matronly giggle, "Sara."

Eric, already regretting his politeness, couldn't shake his good manners, "If you'll please excuse me, I have some work to do."

"Oh, what you need is a cup of coffee." Sara had spotted the Bunn-o-matic when she and Clara entered. She poured from the station's dented, stainless steel 24-cup pot as naturally as if she were pouring at the Hands and Heart garden club meeting.

Just back from a serious run, Eric was beginning to realize that he was going to have to run again, as Sara pirouetted towards him. Even as a child in socially-required dance class, she was never a graceful pirouetter. Time had not been her friend.

Clara recognized this even if Sara didn't. "We can see you're busy; we'll come back some other day," she said, while pulling Sara away toward Gary and his taxi conveniently waiting at the door. All of Lakeville was abuzz about the death of one of those famous writers, and Gary wanted to keep ahead of the gossip curve. He would embellish the story a bit to make it more lively (That would be a pun he could use.), but he knew first he should get a few juicy tidbits from these attractive gals. It wasn't often nowadays that he met women with a bit of heft to them. Most of those writing ladies up at the Prince George looked like the pencils they wrote with. And here they were in his cab. Catching their eyes in the rearview mirror, Gary seized the opportunity. "How about lunch, ladies?"

He correctly interpreted the question marks on their faces. "You pay and I'll supply the local color."

Sara and Clara had been working together too long to need to confer. They were both aware that Gary was a likely source of important information. "How nice of you," Sara replied.

"We'll go to The Consort."

"As in Prince Consort," Clara whispered.

"It's not the San Souci in Cleveland, but I think you'll like it. Their hamburgers are famous from here to Columbus. And maybe a drink of the local brew will help the little grey cells."

Sara and Clara did like it, especially that local brew, Great Lakes beer, a beverage they had never tried before as it can only be exported from Ohio to four other states, none of them on the East Coast. After an hour or so of serious conversation mixed with laughter and abetted by beer and hamburgers, they were ready to return to Prince George House.

A slight delay was caused by their server and the question, "Desert?"

"You talked me into it," replied Clara.

A short, chocolatey time later, the girls were back at the house, discussing the events of the day, so far. Sara was the first to express her unease, "I'm not sure about that Gary. He tells myths as if they were truth and facts as if they were myths. Only one thing he said that I'm sure was the truth"

"What was that?"

"Those really were darn good hamburgers."

Clara smiled at Sara's little joke and said, "It was a fun lunch, but I have to point out to you that even though Gary incorrectly sees us as potential fellow Comrades, he didn't give us a whiff of a clue, my dear Sara."

"I know I might seem a little foolish about that adorable Eric and wrong about learning something from Gary," Sara replied through tense lips, "but I'm not foolish about words. As your writing partner and editor, I tell you—clues don't whiff!"

Chapter Eleven

Wednesday, continued

Hans and Mary Beth planned a different kind of day. They would never liken themselves to Sara, but weren't they, too, a tad more interested in romance than detecting?

In the morning they were true to their professional selves. Hans worked on finally regaining control over his computer; Mary Beth worked on the book she was writing that compared Henry James to E.M. Forster. One section of the book had already been accepted for publication in a journal. The idea that Forster meant his structure of *Where Angels Fear to Tread* to be a partial response to James's *The Ambassadors* had sold itself. But she hadn't completed it yet. For once she couldn't wrap her mind around Forster. Henry James kept intruding. The more she thought about him, the more she felt that her own life was turning into an Ohio version of "Turn of the Screw." Certainly she was living in the up-dated version of James's fictional stately home, Bly, with its "old machicolated square tower" and the same crooked staircase that made the governess pause. The question was, which of James's strange inhabitants of that "castle of romance" was she playing?

In that ambiguous story, played out in a secluded English estate, a mysterious governess and her two precocious charges never resolve the reader's questions of "Who are the good guys?" and "Who are the bad guys?" For Mary Beth, the occupants of Prince George House offered the same conundrum.

At 1 o'clock Mary Beth and Hans separately put their work aside. Hans thought of strategies; Mary Beth of what she would wear. She pulled on her new tight-white jeans and little black knit top before meeting Hans in the entrance hall, as they had planned. For different reasons, they were both looking forward to escaping for the rest of the day. They had decided that the near-by woods would be an idyllic spot for a simple picnic. Fortunately it was within the Lakeville City limits, fulfilling police requirements. Officer Lois had stopped by earlier in the day to warn all of the temporary residents of Prince George House that they could not leave town during the on-going investigation.

Mary Beth and Hans tossed a coin to see who would be driver for the day. Hans won and chose to drive Mary Beth's car. Though it looked like a midget in the world of Jeep Cherokees and Hummers that surrounded it, convertible weather, not size, was the deciding factor. Now all they needed (and quickly secured) were the box lunches they had ordered from Cook. Hans brought a bonus in his canvas carry-all, a decent bottle of Molderbach sauvignon blanc and some paper cups. Another bonus. Hans opened the PT Cruiser's passenger door for Mary Beth, somehow necessitating his putting his arm around her, "You look great in your car, Mary Beth. It fits you perfectly."

Mary Beth smiled.

As he got into his side of the car, he added, "I have a surprise for you, too, Mary Beth."

Mary Beth smiled again.

Then she realized the implications. *Oh, dear*, she thought. *I'm not ready for our relationship to move that quickly.* She guiltily remembered that she was wearing her sexiest, fun Victoria Secret satin thong, complete with sequins. What was she ready for?

She looked at Hans. Even his flip-flops and less-than-stylish sunglasses couldn't conceal how good looking he was. Mary Beth's smile was becoming perpetual.

With their packages in the back seat and Hans taking a turn at the wheel, they set off on their adventure. Hans turned out to be less skillful as a driver than he was as a writer. Mary Beth progressively stiffened as Hans progressively drifted from one side to the other of the (fortunately) deserted road. He was more interested in steering the conversation than the car. "I can't tell you, Mary Beth, how happy I am to get out of that house. Your being with me is a plus. The situation there is way beyond the occasional weirdness that always seeps through ordinary life."

"Well, yes, I'd say murder is more than your ordinary every-day weirdness."

"More than that. I think Malcolm has a unique sense of integrity. He's true to his art, but beyond that, don't you find him a little strange?"

"Who there don't you find a little strange, Hans?"

"Good question," he answered as he pulled into the small car park in front of the woods. "It's a cringeworthy crowd. Forget them. Today is about us. Let's look for a secluded site. It'll hardly be a problem. We seem to be the only car parked here."

"Do you believe in omens?" Mary Beth asked and hurriedly made her point before Hans could take her too seriously. "Look at the sign."

"It just says 'Ohio State Nature Preserve. Oh, I see. The second line says 'Syberling Woods.' That must be our very own Mr. Syberling who gave the land to the State. It does make this outing a tad more *personal*."

Mary Beth internalized that emphasis and started to walk. Hans followed.

Carrying their lunch boxes and Hans's 'magic reticule,' they made their way past stands of White and Northern Red Oak to a quiet, relatively flat area bordered in Flowering Dogwood and Sassafras. "A few weeks earlier and the Dogwoods would have been in bloom, but it's lovely now. What wonderful odors." Mary Beth said.

Hans picked up a handful of dried twigs for her to sniff. "Sassafras. Smells almost like root beer, doesn't it?"

He took a blanket out of his carry-all. Once out of the car, Mary Beth had begun to relax a little, but now, that blanket. *Uh oh,* she thought. She nervously tried to start a conversation out of the raw materials at hand. "Hans, what is that interesting tree with the shaggy gray bark peeling from the trunk? And that lovely one just beginning to bloom with the orange-centered flowers?"

"Mary Beth, that's a Shag Bark Hickory and next to it are some Tulip Trees. What's this sudden interest?

"I myself enjoy the wonders of nature in the abstract," he explained. "I like identifying birds and trees, especially in books. But when you get down that ladder of abstractions to the actual earthy nits and all of this grit, that's what I don't like." Mary Beth wasn't sure if she felt deflated or relieved with the explanation for the blanket. She was to wonder again a few minutes later.

He poured the wine; they munched their chicken sandwiches and chatted. Hans was surprisingly vocal: "It's good to be alone, away from the others, and away from the noise of Nikki's damn cappuccino machine. That Indigo Bunting singing away, even in the middle of the day, is a pleasant change.

"Now for my surprise." He touched her shoulder. Mary Beth took another deep breath.

Chapter Twelve

Wednesday afternoon, continued

Hans took out a wooden box of paints and some white sketch pads. "Do you paint, Mary Beth?"

Mary Beth let out her deep breath and answered, "No. Do you?"

"No, I don't at all. Well, I haven't for a very long time. That's why I thought we would really get away by doing something different, but still creative. I 'borrowed' these paints and sketch pads from Malcolm. I had to kind of sneak into their suite, The Emerson Suite. Wasn't he the philosopher who said, 'Simplify. Simplify?' "

"Actually, I think it was his disciple, Thoreau," Mary Beth gently corrected Hans, while harshly correcting herself, *Why am I being so tentative about being smart? I know it was Thoreau.*

"Well, one of those guys. Malcolm has done the opposite of simplify. Do you know how much photography equipment he has in that electronic cave of his? One wall looks like it's the set for a 'B' sci-fi movie set. Machines and gadgets I don't even recognize. And he has his own processing room tucked inside that mansion. I would have liked to look inside. Digital photography has put darkrooms on the road to extinction. It would have been something to see." Little did Hans guess how much there would have been to see.

Hans continued, "It's almost quaint that he still has a darkroom, especially since I hear he's so involved in the digital part of it. But the red light was on. Even I know what that means."

Hans set out the box of water colors. "We have a couple of ounces of wine left. We can use it to mix paints. Who knows? Maybe we'll be creating a new medium. And maybe the painting will help my mogigraphia."

"What?"

"One synonym for mogigraphia is graphospasm. It's almost a physical writer's block. If you want to be ordinary, it's writers' cramp. But I'd say that you and I are anything but ordinary, Mary Beth."

Mary Beth laughed. It wasn't that Hans was so funny. He really wasn't. But she was happy, happier than she had been since she left Midfield. She realized that she was relieved that the blanket and the surprise didn't involve sex. She liked Hans. She liked the box lunch and the sauvignon blanc. She liked the woods and the idea of painting them. She liked . . . NO. She pushed Tony and Midfield out of her mind and concentrated on her art. The two amateurs painted quietly and intently. Mary Beth was making the discovery that she enjoyed playing with colors. She could see the similarities to playing with words, especially when she tried to get the exact color she wanted. *That green isn't right*, she thought. She reached out for some grasses and rubbed them across the paper. That's the right shade. "Oh, sorry. I spilled the blue. Serendipitous. It looks good."

"Yes. You've created a fine landscape with all of those greens and blues. I can almost see a Yellow Warbler hiding there." He pointed. "Funny, all of that turbulence in your earth and sky is in direct contrast to mine. Look. It's Mondrian-inspired using twigs and paint in straight intersecting lines. You know, before I turned to writing, I studied with Harry Holzman, a disciple of Mondrian's and the executor of his will. But I broke with Harry because of my need for more tools for emotional expression."

'A fine landscape'? What earth and sky? Is he being patronizing just because I spilled some blue paint over green grass? There's something about his social skills. He just doesn't get it. Or doesn't want to. And if those rigid lines are his idea of emotional expression,

maybe I don't want to get him. Or maybe I still do. She smiled to herself, a smile that Hans thought was directed to him.

He returned the smile, thinking: *Mary Beth is having a fine time. Almost like a child playing. I'm enjoying the afternoon, too, though I'm not a child. I play more adult games.*

Hans wasn't ready to drop the potential of a relationship with Mary Beth or even to drop the conversation. "Look at my finger," he said, pointing to a slight redness. "We've just been out in this natural world for an hour or so and I have some kind of an allergic rash. It's a contact dermatitis I picked up someplace. How do you suppose I provoked Mother Nature?"

"She must have heard you say that you didn't like her actual nits and grits."

Hans turned back to their paintings, "Our art work is more than O.K. for beginners, but in the rest of our Lakeville world, there's more than my finger that doesn't look good. I said it to you earlier and I'll say it again: an essential strangeness pervades the whole scene."

"Didn't anyone like Marian? Everyone seemed to stiffen when she entered the room."

"Well, Mary Beth, we know that someone there didn't like Marian."

"To be honest, before I met her, I could have been that someone. I came to Lakeville prepared to dislike her intensely. In fact, I wanted to show her up. But that's not exactly the same as murder. A long time ago, she stole (That's not the right word) seduced, (No guy really gets seduced). Anyhow, she hit on and won the boyfriend of one of my best friends in Midfield. I don't know his name, but hers is Dr. Abby Mackenzie. You wouldn't know her. She's not a writer, but she's been like the sister I never had."

Oh, but I do know her, Hans thought. Touching Mary Beth on the arm for assurance, he told her, "I'm that guy, the villain in your little script. Marian and I had a long relationship that I am not going to discuss. And before that, Abby and I were, as you might be apt to say, an item. You know what, my dear, our whole friendship, yours and mine, is beginning to look something like incest." Hans punctuated his statement by leaning over to give her a kiss on the cheek, rather paternally, she thought.

In return she had a slightly vindictive pleasure in saying, "Abby and Amos, her extremely meaningful other, are in Peru right now. With her medical background and his interest in alpaca farming, they're planning to develop some new breeds and revolutionize the field, first in Ohio, then nationally."

"Mary Beth, that's over. You don't have to defend Abby to me."

Hans was right. As they packed up their belongings to go back to Prince George House, Mary Beth was trying to figure out the situation: *So he's Abby's mysterious 'H.T.' She never would tell me his name. Well, he is a hunk. It would be something to be seen at theater openings and book launches with him. But those paintings told me a lot. Worse, he was the guy who dumped Abby? How could I go out with him—even if there was a little spark? Maybe it was just at the beginning.*

So, on varying levels of dissatisfaction, Mary Beth and Hans left the woods, on some levels more knowledgeable than they had been, but strangely just as curious about each other as when they had entered.

They followed a different trail on their way out and were rewarded by seeing an area joyously blanketed by blue and white blue-eyed Marys. But then, a mockingbird signaled their departure. *Another omen?* wondered Mary Beth.

The first thing Mary Beth saw when she returned to her room was Marian's shawl still draped over her bedside chair. She picked it up; it was cold, dramatic, yet lovely—the way Marian had been in death and, to go by all reports, in life, too. Before Marian had been killed, the biggest mystery about her was the obvious conflict between her life and her work. How could anyone so devoid of normal caring emotions write books that children and their parents loved? Somehow, she did. Mary Beth chastised herself for thinking negatively about someone who had just died. After all, this was Ohio where the glass was always half full. She tried to think positively, and recalled Marian's loaning her the shawl, a spontaneous act of friendship. Her affection for Marian and her interest in solving the homicide were re-kindled.

But before getting back to detecting, she had some housekeeping work to do. Mary Beth took out the bankbook and checks she had brought along in the hopes of someday balancing. They were becoming a permanent part of her luggage. She looked at them, put them back in her suitcase and turned to her computer. She decided to play with e-mail before going to work in "documents." New mail showed a message from Tony. Again, how did he know what she was doing or with whom? Tony had many sides; he was an engineer, a bicycle repair man, and a quotation collector, but he was not a clairvoyant.

"I've been thinking about this separation, Mary Babe. Even though it's for such a short time, I think maybe I'm missing you or is it what Thomas Campbell says, 'Tis distance lends enchantment to the view/And robes the mountains in its azure hue.' That's what your friend Mr. Forster does, doesn't he in *Passage to India* – gives a distant then a close-up view of Chandrapore? But I was thinking of you. I do sometimes. T."

audrey lavin

Chapter Thirteen

Wednesday, continued

The picnic that Mary Beth and Hans had naively considered their own affair had been closely studied by various denizens of the closed society that currently comprised Prince George House.

From his leaded window, Buck watched with a writer's eye for detail as his co-writers returned. He noted that though they walked side by side from Mary Beth's car to the house, they didn't occasionally, quite accidentally, touch as they had on leaving.

If they're just going to be friends, they're the investigative group I'll join up with, he decided. *I know it was murder, and it would look awfully suspicious if I was the only one not searching for the killer. It might even seem strange if I didn't want to share any clues or ideas with a group. In this crowd, trying to solve the crime solo would bring as much trouble as ignoring it would. It'd be like breaking a bronco in the rodeo without a pick-up man.* Buck often kept up his cowboy veneer even with an audience of one, himself.

Buck sorted through the possibilities of other pairings. *I could link up with those cozy dames in their velour warm-up suits. They've got some smarts hidden behind those Clara and Sara façades. Look at all of the money they've made writing books. But they probably wouldn't want an outsider. Even me.*

And I certainly can't be a party to anything Nikki and that dude Malcolm are up to. Nikki knows what a cowpoke likes all right. He allowed himself a reminiscent grin. *But then she opens her mouth. I don't think she can utter a sentence without a cliché in it. How can he*

*stand it? By now all I can say to her is, "My, you're purty, ma'am."
But as she would say, "I shouldn't be the one to throw a stone unless I
lived in a glass house."*

*I think I'm stronger than Mary Beth and Hans. I can ride with
them. I'd easily be the trail boss and still have time to get some work
done. That's what I came here for.*

Buck went downstairs to corral Mary Beth and Hans or, would he
lasso them as they entered the corral of Prince George House? Buck
edited and rewrote his thoughts as carefully as he edited and rewrote his
novels. He had to in order to keep his Western mask from slipping. It
did a good job of protecting him from the world and from himself.

Sara and Clara, back from their interview with Eric, were watching
from their leaded window, too.

"Does she look mussed up to you?"

"Sorry to say, no, not a dirty blond hair out of place."

"Well, I'll bet they weren't out there bird watching for new species
to add to their life list," Clara countered.

"Whatever they were up to on their so-called 'picnic,' they missed
all of the news here." Sara compressed her lips, "Wait until they see
today's *Daily Record* with its 'Poison Pen' headlines and story about
Marian. Murder confirmed. At least the coroner says he's eliminated
all natural causes; his full report will be out soon. Bad news sure does
travel fast."

"Come on, Sara, Mary Beth and Hans are smart enough to have
guessed what that news would be when Detective Lois stopped by with
her 'Don't leave town' warning."

"But, Clara, did they have to run bios on all of us under 'Writers'
Wacky World?' "

"Look at it as good publicity for our next book. How could the
paper be talking about poison when she looked so neat? I swear she
looked like a mannequin in a department store window. When we write
a book all of the people who are poisoned have some kind of
convulsions."

"That part about poison was complete speculation. They don't even have the full coroner's report yet. I'm sure a toxicology report takes longer."

"Look, Sara, police. Right after Mary Beth and Hans went into the house, a guy wearing fancy sunglasses rode up on a black bicycle. He must be delivering something. See that police car that passed him; it's parking in front of the house. We're having a regular parade. But no sirens. I guess they aren't going to arrest any of us." She nibbled on her bottom lip, "Maybe they have something to tell us."

The tall, lean man the girls were watching dismounted from his new Cannondale R5000 bike, gave the speedometer a "well-done" pat, and stopped to talk with the police. By then, Mary Beth was at her window, too, and realized who the cyclist was. She ran down the steps and out of the door to greet him. She stopped. This was a confusing surprise. Should she be angry because he hadn't told her he was coming or happy because he was here?

She hadn't realized how much she had missed Tony. *But I'm not going to let him know,* she decided as she advanced more slowly. *It wasn't the weeks apart. That was nothing. It was his attitude towards it, his wanting time apart. That was something. Too much!* She gave him a welcoming, but carefully friendly hug.

His return hug was on a more personal level. Mary Beth had forgotten how strong Tony's arms were. She remembered.

The other writers politely nodded at Tony Bartlett when introduced, though Buck made a point of giving him a crushing handshake, "Ah comes from out West where the handshakes and life are a little stronger," he said.

Tony responded with a sweeping salutation, "Buck and all of you writers, I salute you with admiration. As Ezra Pound said, 'Literature is news that *stays* news.' " This raised some eyebrows as no one but Mary Beth was familiar with Tony's conversational style that lapsed at times into the quotations he was editing for his still unpublished reference book, *Bartlett's BETTER Quotations.* But his potential audience's concentration was not on any greeting of his, rather on the possibility of hearing some hard news from Lois and Co.

As they moved toward their news source, Mary Beth and Tony were left alone. Mary Beth wasn't ready for this. She leaped in with a question, forcing possibly awkward conversation into a safe channel. "I see you're riding a new bike, Tony. What happened to your Paramount—and all the time you spent adding those recycled Campo, Campo-something parts?"

"Campognola, Mary Beth. I upgraded. Like my new Cannondale? It's a blast. My old bike was excellent but heavier; this one has an aluminum frame instead of a steel one. Really cool, isn't it? It's equipped with Dura Ace components, too."

Mary Beth fidgeted, *That's what I get for asking. We've got to move off of this subject before I get the history of each component part.* She led Tony closer to the group gathered around Lois.

Lois was telling the assembled writers to go for a walk or into the garden while the police team made a house search. A sharp "No" greeted Malcolm's request that he go to his rooms to retrieve just a few necessary items. "This 'No' isn't just for you, Malcolm. No one can take any thing out of the house except what is on your body now, and each of you will be lightly searched as you leave the house."

Nikki giggled. "At the end of the day, groping is—well, groping is . . . " She realized that she was out of sync. Everyone else realized that she was out of sync. Everyone else was grumbling.

Everyone except Buck. *That lady is one good cop,* he thought. *I'll bet if I could get her alone, she'd be one terrific bad cop, too.*

But Sara and Clara were complaining, "Invasion of privacy. Searched?

Is that really necessary?"

Even Tony asked, "Should we be lawyering-up?"

Hans asked a more pertinent question, "Do you have a warrant?"

"Yes, we have a warrant. We also have warrants to search your electronics. We know your good hosts, Nikki and Malcolm, provided each guest with a PC; we take it for granted that some of you brought your laptops. I'm sure you all have cell phones, too. We can check those out later. Ernie, our tech expert, has already powered down Marian's computer. He'll be pulling the power cords on the rest of you, even as we speak. We want to quarantine all of the machines ASAP. Fair warning. Ernie is a computer forensics investigator. He can retrieve information that has been deleted or written over, so don't bother running up to your rooms for a last minute cover-up."

"What about fingerprints?" Mary Beth asked.

"So far, we've had no results from the items we originally bagged from Marian's room, nothing from the box of candy or the book she was reading. Nothing unusual about the clothes you identified as being what she wore yesterday. Some fingerprints were found on the doorknob but no fingerprints except for Marian's were in the room. There, I give you people who discovered her credit. You were careful not to touch anything.

"No obvious poison or suspicious objects, either. Since the coroner has eliminated natural causes and no blows or wounds are visible, we're looking into an arcane poison of some kind. Blood, hair, and skin samples are in the state lab right now with a duplicate package on its way to the Poison Center. We'll be getting a rushed toxicology report tomorrow. And I'll be double checking all of the trash then, too." Lois allowed herself an unprofessional, "Ugh!"

Amidst the grumbling and shifting of positions, only Malcolm seemed to have a purpose. It was a very simple one: to bring some order out of chaos. If he couldn't control anything else, he could control room assignments. "Tony," he called, "do you have a minute?"

"Of course, sir," said Tony not yet sure of everyone's name. "What is it?"

"By now this isn't exactly the uninterrupted retreat Nikki and I had planned. We wouldn't normally allow non-participants to stay here. But if you'll stay out of the way of creativity, you can use a guest room here for the rest of the week. You're welcome to a back room." He hurried on with his explanation. "It's part of the servants' quarters from Prince George's days of greater glory. We've been working on restoration, especially the wiring of that part of the house." He smiled "But some rooms are quite livable."

"Sold! I mean, thank you, sir. I'll take it. I won't even bother checking it out until later."

At that point, six curious or angry people plus two very worried ones filed out into the garden. Some sat on the garden benches, some walked around bumping into their colleagues, stepping aside for them on the narrow, authentically antique-brick paths. "Excuse me."

"No, excuse me."

The third time this interchange took place between Tony and Hans, Tony, who was quick to recognize a rival, bristled: "In Bill's own words, 'And oftentimes excusing of a fault/doth make the fault the worse by the excuse.'"

Clara, amused by the near-confrontation, tried to defuse the atmosphere. She turned to Sara and said, "What a pleasant place to walk. I love long walks, don't you?"

Sara responded, directing her eyes toward Hans and Tony, "Especially when they are taken by people who annoy me."

Clara smothered her laughter.

Hans was trying a little defusing of his own, "Come on, Tony. We're all a little tense." Then, with a slightly guilty conscience based on his fantasy life, he added, "You've just been here a short time, though I can see that it's been long enough to pick up gossip. *Alors*, no matter what any of the resident overly-observant scribes has told you, I do not, I repeat, I do not have designs on your girlfriend."

On over-hearing this, Mary Beth felt an unreasonable tendency toward hurt feelings. *Didn't I decide that I wasn't interested? That I didn't care? What do I care what Hans says? Or can I be interested in two men in the same way at the same time?* Conflicting thoughts buzzed through her head. But she hid her emotions from her colleagues by keeping her confusion-filled visage turned to her note taking.

She was interrupted by Nikki's taking the seat next to her on the bench. "Mary Beth, I've wanted to ask you something important," Nikki confided.

Maybe this is it, a break through, Mary Beth thought. "What is it Nikki?" she asked in her fake-sincerest voice.

"Well, I've been wondering about what you do with matzah."

"What?"

"Yes, I've been wondering. I want to serve it in your honor, but at the end of the day, I have to say it's the only food I've ever tried that tastes exactly like the box it comes in. Oh, you'll have to tell me later. Malcolm is signaling he wants to talk with me. Ta ta."

Mary Beth pulled herself together and tried to go back to her work. She was somewhat distracted by the bees humming around the wall of beautiful white hydrangeas on the far side of the path. She learned later that the hydrangeas were not original to the house, but had been planted over 50 years ago and had grown to make a dramatic fence for one side of the garden. *If only the bees didn't accompany it.*

She started to list clues and forgot for a while where she was when Officer Lois's arrival startled her out of her concentration. *Isn't it strange that Lois is carrying packages of videos under her arm?* Mary Beth wasn't the only one who noticed. A buzz similar to that of the bees could be heard. It consisted of phrases like, "Now what's up?" and "Entertainment for tonight?"

Lois ignored the buzz and announced, "You can all go back into the house now, but remember, the don't-leave-town rule still holds. What I mean is that you all can return to your quarters—except for your hosts Nikki and Malcolm. You two had better come to the station with me."

audrey lavin

Chapter Fourteen

Wednesday, continued

The strangest part of this request was that although both Nikki and Malcolm's faces visibly blanched, they did not object. In fact, Malcolm turned so that all could hear his indignant defense of what he considered to be the motivational "art" behind the accusation of criminal intent that he knew was imminent. "Why am I being persecuted?" he asked his gape-faced colleagues. "I designed these works to fill the space between the subconscious libido and the interactive arts environment."

"What the hey are you talking about?" Buck had no hesitation in shouting out the question that was on everyone's mind.

"I am following my muse," Malcolm tried to explain to the law officers and his guests. "By splicing and digitalizing the video frames of your sometimes esoteric activities, I have created a new art form. I even manipulated your faces so none of you could sue me. And by the time I finished, who would want to? Which one of you would want to admit being a part of my work that crosses new erotic borders?"

"What erotic borders?" Buck spoke for all again. "I've got my passport at the ready." He'd gone too far again.

Meanwhile, the situation was becoming frighteningly clear: Malcolm had been using criminal means to create his art works. Criminal means that impinged on the lives of his supposed guests. At the least, they were told, he had been systematically violating their privacy to achieve his "great" artistic ends.

It seemed that Nikki had gone along. *It's more than possible*, Mary Beth thought, *that she doesn't have a clue. With all of her girly-girl posturing, potential pornography wouldn't be in the script she thought she was writing for her life.*

She realized that Hans was subtly nudging her. "That darkroom. I should have explored it," he whispered as if they were fellow conspirators.

"What about me?" Mary Beth asked. "I should have realized from what you were describing that something was more than a little bit off. So much for my career as Mary Beth Goldberg, girl investigator."

Buck held up his hands in denial. He was trying to wipe out the entire scene. "Hombres," he said "that is as far into ugly territory as I want to explore." He thought for a minute: "If they planned to sell our pictures, at least I'm physically fit," he informed the stunned writers.

He wouldn't stop: "I don't even have to do stretches. In fact, even in my rodeo days, my idea of a stretch was sitting on a tailgate, reaching for a beer."

Ignoring his tasteless comments, Sara shook her head, "It's just wrong. Very wrong," she said.

In the background, Mary Beth could hear Lois start to give Malcolm and Nikki their Miranda rights, "I am a Police Officer. I warn you that . . ." And she heard Nikki cut in, "Oh, I know you're a Police Officer." Mary Beth was right. Nikki really didn't get it. After the Mirandizing process was completed, the two culprits were walked to the car waiting to take them to the police station.

As she passed Mary Beth, Nikki stopped and looked at her for a minute, "As your people would say, 'Never take a front seat at a bris.' " Maybe she had understood more than she let on.

"The rest of you stay away from the Haverfords' quarters," Lois directed. "Their suite is out-of-bounds. That means no one goes into Nikki or Malcolm's bedroom, studio, bathroom or office. In case any one forgets that simple order, I'm having more yellow tape put on all of their exterior doors."

Buck's thoughts drifted from the criminals to the policewoman: *She's a feisty one,* he thought, *just like my lusty, busty Rusty. In my next chapter, I ought to get Rusty (maybe Lois?) to a rodeo. You work up a certain level of excitement when you're there and the adrenalin starts going. It's all reaction. You've just gotta let your body go.* He chuckled to himself, *That would be a good way to get Rusty (maybe Lois?) to move on to the next man.*

In unspoken agreement with each other, Clara and Sara abruptly turned from the group, retreating to their room for the needed strength they always found in reinforced coffee.

A short time later at the police station, Malcolm was booked on felony charges of burglary and wire tapping plus possession of criminal tools. He and Nikki were also charged with the misdemeanor of voyeurism.

Back at the house, the five writers and even Tony, who didn't know the presumed-guilty pair, were in a state of shock over the arrest. They were more shocked when they learned the charges, including the fact that a part of their personal lives had been burglarized. As Officer Lois later explained, the criminal tools referred to were a wireless video camera and transmitter hidden in the hub of the winged fan in each bedroom. The policewoman said, "The television and VCR set-ups to receive the fan-videos were found in Malcolm's studio during the house search for clues to Marian's death. Plus, when we started to search their computers, we found that those people I'd previously referred to as 'your good hosts' had a suspicious amount of graphic image manipulation software. That's not the crime. It was what they did with the software. Do you understand that all of you have been taped without your knowledge?" This was a question that concentrated attention.

"That Malcolm's a bottom-feeder," said Hans.

"Literally," smiled Tony and turned to Mary Beth.

"Mary-Babe, do you understand that every time you walked into your room and turned on the light, you activated the ceiling fan?"

"I've been here for three days, Tony. I'm not dense. Even though you're the engineer, of course, I noticed."

"That also means that every time you activated the fan, you turned on the camera, so your friendly publican could watch you. You and everybody else here."

Mary Beth's face also blanched. *Thank goodness I've been leading an innocent life here. They couldn't hold secretly eating a bag full of chocolate covered marshmallows against me.* She laughed at herself.

Stepping into the garden and pulling Mary Beth along with him, Tony said, "There's too much group togetherness here for me, but now that we have a minute alone, I brought you a present."

"A present?" *How un-Tony,* she thought. "How wonderful," she said.

Tony took a folded document out of his back pocket: McCollege's literary journal, or to be exact *Midfield Campus College's Collected Treasures Sweet* (the title an obscure allusion to the work of Thomas Gray forced on the department by Hake, its chair.) "Look at the cover, Mary Best."

Sure enough, next to the title of Mary Beth's contribution to the journal was a small blurred snapshot of her.

"A gift, though small, is precious," Tony said and added "that's from Homer's *Odyssey*. I'm thinking of including it in my *Bartlett's BETTER Quotations* book."

Mary Beth was studying the journal. "Wow, I'm almost a campus celebrity. One caveat. No one reads the journal. But it's a forecast of future fame. From the cover of *M.C.C's Collected Treasures Sweet*, it's bound to be a direct trajectory to being a *People* cover girl. Thanks, Tony."

"I'd say a *Playboy* centerfold," he laughed.

An hour later, Officer Lois returned to Prince George House and assembled the still unbelieving writers. Who would have guessed that a cursory room search for clues to one crime would turn up a crime against all of them?

Some, more than others, had a difficult time understanding Lois's explanation of what the police hoped to gain from the arrest of their hosts: prosecution of Nikki and Malcolm, of course. But also expectations were high that Malcolm's film would show Marian's murderer caught in the act or possibly entering or leaving the room. Even if the videotapes didn't contain specific evidence, the police were sure that they would offer important clues. Lois explained to the assembled writers that they were required to stay in Lakeville and continue to live in Prince George House. "You are permitted to go into the village, but must sign in and out on the sheet I am putting on that old rectory table in the entrance hall. Everyone understand?" she added.

Tony listened with Mary Beth and the other deflated authors to Lois's pronouncements. He looked extremely doubtful as she made her last request. Crouching down to talk to Mary Beth in what he thought was a muted voice, he said, "Do you think someone who has just committed a murder is going to hesitate to lie about what time he–or she," he amended seeing *that* look cross her face. "Do you think a murderer would necessarily be truthful about his or her comings and goings? What is Officer Lois thinking?

"Geesh, Mary Best, I thought coming to visit you would be like what Annie Dillard said about Key West, 'The wonderful thing about Prince George House is that you get to hang around with other people who are spending their days at such an absurd task as writing.' And here I get to hang around with people in the middle of a bizarre murder and this creepy invasion of privacy. But I'm sure the murder will be solved soon."

"Inşhallah."

"What's that?"

"Oh, I used to say it in Turkey. It's kind of a short-hand for our Ohio saying, 'If the good Lord's willin' and the crick don't rise.' "

"O.K. Give me a minute, Mary Babe." Tony ran upstairs to unpack his luggage. Tony traveled light—for a few days at Lakeville or last summer's cross-country bike trip, luggage consisted of a backpack that contained his second and identical outfit of black jeans and black T- shirt. It also contained his good-luck cycling jersey. He started to put it on, then decided he didn't need it—yet. He took another minute or two to struggle with the window in order to let some fresh air in and the musty smell of disuse out.

By an unspoken, common consent, the writers had trooped into the library. Tony joined them a few minutes later. With his book-in progress, *Bartlett's BETTER Quotations: Quotes You'll Use Every Day,* he counted himself as an equal member of the creative group.

Then . . . the realization that had been on the edge of everyone's consciousness sunk in. They were all suspect. By now it was real. Each person there understood that one of them actually could be the murderer. Mary Beth looked around. Hans, Buck, Sara, Clara, and Tony were looking around, too, directly or furtively.

If a room can bristle with tension, this one did. It was a good time, as they say, to leave.

Chapter Fifteen

later Wednesday

Dinner was forgotten—even by Cook who could not believe that she had watched her employers being led away by the police. Had the Revolution started? She retreated to her herb garden. Other residents of Prince George house had similar reactions.

Mary Beth suddenly wanted to write something she had just thought of about Forster and James. Hans and Buck remembered a pub in town they meant to visit for local color. Tony decided to explore the house. As a newcomer, he wanted to get his bearings. Plus, his Ph. D. in engineering had led him to a peripheral interest in architecture. Prince George House piqued his intellectual curiosity. Sara and Clara needed to get something (medicinal) from their room, but before they went upstairs, they let everyone know that they intended to persevere with their investigation.

The public announcement of their intent to continue detecting had been made to put them on record as being on the good side of the crime. Once in their room, Sara filled two cups from the carafe of coffee, another of the amenities of Ohio Creates, and fortified them. Sipping their enhanced coffee, Sara and Clara talked over their actual plans. "Where can we search for clues in this place? So much black fingerprint dust is around that we'll leave footprints (She almost said "paw prints") wherever we go. Anyway, half of the house is cordoned off with crime scene tape."

Clara nodded her head knowingly, "Maybe we won't have to. I was sure M&M's weren't so sweet. Their holier-than-thou-will-ever-be attitude was so phony. Now that they've been arrested, everyone's going to think they did her in."

"M&M? They say hearing is the first thing to go. That is Nikki and Malcolm. Not Mickie and Malcolm."

Clara watched. *Yes.* Sara pursed her lips in annoyance. She was going to give Clara another lecture. "Get your mind away from your candy bars, Clara. Even I can see that you're getting to be one fat cat."

"Humph," Clara cleverly replied. She knew that sarcasm made Sara feel comfortable. Except when she was writing, it was her normal medium. She ignored her writing partner's comment to say, "Let's try to see Lois. She won't tell us anything over the phone, but maybe we can learn something if we see her in person." She accompanied her suggestion with punching in Officer Lois's phone number to ask her for an appointment.

"It's after hours, so I have a free twenty minutes right now and that's it," Lois said. Lakeville is a small town. Sara and Clara, taking time to finish their drinks, hailed the omnipresent Gary and were at the police station in a little over ten minutes.

Officer Lois didn't really have a 'free' twenty minutes. She never did. This was just an evening slot that wasn't filled with appointments. While Clara and Sara sat at the visitor's side of her desk, the FAX machine on the working side generated pages faster than the attached receptacle could contain them. Lois reached out to catch them with her left hand. Her right hand was otherwise occupied taking notes from a voice coming over the phone receiver she was precariously holding under her chin. The faxes and the phone call were from Lois's late-working contacts at the Poison Center. When she finally put the phone down, Lois explained to the impressed on-lookers, "This is going to be in tomorrow's *Lakeville Ledger* anyway, so I might as well tell you. I'm going to skip all of the legal and forensic gobbledygook," she said, pointing to the faxed papers, many of which were now on the floor. "As we had suspected, the official cause of Marian's death is poison administered by a person or persons unknown. The poison itself is unrecognized at this time, but further tests are being conducted."

"Cook. In the kitchen," was Clara's immediate response, thinking of food again. "Poison is definitely a cook's weapon. And our cook has her private herb garden. If you ask me, ..."

Lois cut her short: "Cook is one of the few people in that house who have been completely cleared. She and a local cab driver . ."

"Gary from Indiana?" asked Sara.

"For amateur detectives, you ladies are pretty darn good. Yes, Gary. He and Cook were at their Marxist criticism group until the wee hours of the night."

"What about Nickie and Malcolm? Are they involved in the murder too?" asked Sara.

"No more information," Lois said getting up from her desk.

"One last question. Can we tell the others about the poison?" Sara asked as Lois dismissed them for the evening.

"Be my guest. Everyone's gonna' know in a couple of hours."

Clara and Sara had the waiting taxi rush them back to Prince Albert House. "Before we tell the others, let's explore the kitchen," Sara suggested.

Clara agreed, "Good idea. We can scrounge a late supper AND be on the cutting edge of this investigation. Tomorrow we can tell the others that we've already searched for poisonous substances."

"The others" weren't hanging around the house waiting to get their news from Clara and Sara. Buck and Hans, for two, were talking quietly while they ate shepherd's pie and drank Newcastle Brown ale from imitation old tankards at the Consort Pub. "It would be better straight from the bottle, but at least it's not French," was Buck's summation of the Lakeville beer scene.

"What do you think is going on at the house?" Hans asked him.

"I don't know, but I've always had a hankerin' for a roan filly."

"I kind of like the amateur gumshoe myself," Hans smiled in reply, but turned the conversation back to his original subject, "Do you think the two crimes are connected, the video voyeurism and the macabre murder?"

Buck helped himself to a handful of peanuts, "I may wear glasses, but I can still see the sun at noon-day and that connection's so bright it durn near flashes at you. How can you have two crimes in one house in one week and not have them related?"

"D'accord, my fine Western friend, though I've never before believed in multi-tentacled conspiracy theories. You know I can't get over Marian's death." He added a quick disclaimer, "Of course, I barely knew her."

Buck looked him in the eye, "You're talking about both meanings of the word?"

Hans turned away. "O.K, that's it." Time to get a little writing done now. We can confer this evening with the rest of our crime-solving team about Nikki and Malcolm. It's suspicious enough that they're each other's alibis."

"So are those cozy gals. At least that's what they told me."

"What? They're Nikki and Malcolm's alibis?"

"No, each other's alibis."

"Well, for that matter, I'll bet the rest of us are, too. Each other's alibis, that is."

"Not that guy Tony. He wasn't here. He's the only one who didn't even know Marian."

"No, not Tony. But you and Mary Beth and even I."

"That kinda' makes me break trail with a sobering idea, podner. It's not only that everyone has an alibi. Maybe it's that when you git down to the bottom of the hay rick, no one has an alibi."

They weren't the only ones de-constructing the crimes. Oppressed by the house and the situation, Mary Beth had gone through the French doors into the garden for the cooler air of the evening. That was the right decision. There was Tony exploring the grounds. Mary Beth ran over to him, spilling out words as she approached. "I have to tell you, Tony, I had cast Nikki and Malcolm as the children Flora and Miles in *Turn of the Screw*. But in James's story we never know if the children are the evil guilty ones or the innocent victims. Here they certainly are the guilty ones. At least of one crime.

"Mary Best, you know I wouldn't be here now if I didn't care about you, but delete it. What in the world does your literary analysis have to do with anything? You sound like you're turning into that wildly delusional children's governess in *The Screw*."

"You were smart to preface that remark with a compliment, Tony. I'll skip the governess crack. You almost hoisted yourself there by your own pony-tail. As to what does *Turn of the Screw* have to do with anything? Nothing. But remember, I'm an academic and very good at making footnotes."

"To be fair, Mary Best, you do have something in common with your friend, the English governess. If you accept her story, she's kind of a detective investigating what happened to the children—and hey, I'm on a roll here. You know that other book you're always talking about, James's *The Ambassadors*? That ambassador-guy was doing a lot of investigating, too. So your books really have some connection with what we're doing now.

"Maybe with this house, too. I've only had time to give it a cursory look, Mary Babe, but what I've seen is that it's deceiving. It's not only a residence, it's a fortress."

"That's *Turn of the Screw* again, Tony. You're right. When I talk with my class about the stately homes of England, like the one in the book, I try to explain the role these houses play in their owners' lives. I always credit the critic Mark Spilka with saying that the large house where the English governess works is 'supposed to be a defensive reaction against inroads on family life.' "

"Yeah, Tony added, "and a seat of power, too. Look what happened to Malcolm when he began to occupy that seat. The power went straight to his spy-ware. He thought he could get away with anything." Tony, never one to create a new epigram when an old one would do, brought the house discussion to an end, "As Lord Acton said 'Power tends to corrupt,' and I say it doesn't have to be absolute power to corrupt absolutely.

"But, look, enough analyzing. O.K.? I need some time off, Mary Babe. I got here a couple of hours ago. I had to meet all of these new people. Then I find they're all murder suspects and I have to assess them. Then I see two of them, your hosts, being arrested for what? Quasi-pornography? And I'm trying to understand the physical lay of the land. It's too much too fast. The worst part is that everyone's stupid ideas are coming at me so quickly that they're having a Doppler Effect on me." Tony put his hands over his ears to emphasize his point. "I can't think straight," he added.

"I know. I need some down-time, too. It's only Wednesday? I feel as if I've been here at least a week. I'll tell Hans and Buck and The Girls that we should all take the rest of the day off from the 'Ohio Creates' routine. We'll take a rest and re-group tomorrow. You've never seen me as the model of a professional authority figure, Tony, but here I'm THE teacher. They'll follow my suggestion. Then you and I can get away without any social eruptions. Besides, I think that's what everyone wants to do."

Mary Beth was right. Hans spoke for all of them when he responded, "Good idea. It's early days yet. We need some time and perspective."

"We can form a real posse in the morning; we'll meet at the chuck wagon," Buck added.

When Mary Beth returned to her Henry James room, Tony followed. First he cleared the blocked threshold of the room by picking up the books and papers Mary Beth had dropped. Once the doorway was cleared, Tony turned toward the corridor and said loudly enough for those listening in the Melville Room to hear, "What happens in Lakeville, stays in Lakeville." Then he closed and locked Mary Beth's bedroom door.

Chapter Sixteen

Thursday

Thursday morning Mary Beth woke happy that she and Tony were together again. Still, she found herself hoping that Hans would be waiting for her at breakfast. *What's happening to me?* she wondered. *My good-girl image is getting a little tarnished around the edges.*

At 8 a.m., a combination of the bright Ohio sunlight coming through the blinds, a harsh knock on each door, and a brusque "downstairs in ten minutes" provided the official wake-up call for the inhabitants of the Melville and other guest rooms. Half asleep, Hans the theater-maven, at first thought he was hearing a stage call.

It was a strange stage that greeted him when he entered the formal sitting room a few minutes after the other writers had assembled. Mary Beth, Sara, Clara, and Buck were seated in front of the coffee table where Cook had arranged a continental breakfast of juice, coffee, tea, and muffins. Gone was the lavish dining-room display of previous mornings. Tony stood center stage, blueberry muffin in hand. No longer a visitor, he was starting to feel at home. Tony had decided during the night that wherever Mary Beth was living would be home to him—though he wasn't sure how to tell Mary Beth about it. Now he was doing what Tony did best when feeling "at home." Using his muffin for emphasis, he was declaiming, "If John Donne were here he would be saying, 'And now good morrow to our waking souls, which watch not one another out of fear.' "

Officer Lois heard the end of Tony's speech as she entered the room. "We should be fearing someone here. Last night someone in this house broke into Nikki and Malcolm's quarters."

Mary Beth and Tony exchanged glances. They were each other's alibis for the entire night. Hans noticed and understood the quick looks, but felt he was still a contender.

Clara and Sara exchanged glances. They were each other's alibis.

Hans and Buck exchanged glances. Buck was the obvious spokesperson for their group of two, "Hans and I were in the library until after 11. Then we went upstairs. I would have heard him if he left his bunk to look for that tramp Marian, and I'm sure he would have heard me, too, but everyone knows I wouldn't get near her with a ten-foot rail-post."

"Right," Lois said, "so none of you did it. Well, maybe you six innocents can help the Lakeville police solve this crime. First of all, thank you for going to headquarters and being fingerprinted. As a result, the Crime Lab has identified all latent fingerprints on the brass door knob and plate of the Haverford's quarters. Each one of you, except for you, Mary Beth and Tony, has entered or come close to entering their rooms. The prints might simply be elimination prints, ones we would expect to find with no relationship to the crime. On the other hand. . ."

Lois addressed her next remark to Mary Beth and Tony, "That doesn't mean you two are beyond suspicion. It just means you didn't leave any prints in the room. Maybe it just means that you're smarter than the average author here."

"How could I have left prints; I've never been in their rooms," Mary Beth replied. She thought back to the picnic. *Yes. Hans had been in the rooms the day before to "borrow" the paints. That might be a hard story to sell.*

But Hans was already talking privately in the corner to one of the policemen who had come in with Lois. The policeman smiled knowingly at Mary Beth.

Out in the hallway, in front of his personal Stetson hat stand, better known as Mr. Syberstone's statue, Buck was holding court. He spoke up, as usual more loudly than was necessary, to Lois, who was taking notes. "I did go into that bedroom, Miss Detective Lois. It was at Nikki's invitation. The little lady wanted some company while Malcolm was out. She's got a body that was worth taking a risk for once, but that so-called mind of hers kept me from ever returning to the well."

Sara and Clara bustled importantly across the room to the hall where Buck and Lois were having their not-so-private conversation. They, too, had important information about the case.

Mary Beth pulled Tony aside, "Look at Clara. Doesn't she think she's the cat's pajamas?"

Tony guffawed. It was an over-reaction to what at any other time wouldn't be much of a joke. But in the extraordinary circumstances of living and working at the site of what now appeared to be three crimes (murder, theft of personal property or identity, and breaking into a crime scene) Mary's Beth's tension breaker was welcomed. Hans, who had left the policeman for Mary Beth's more interesting company, gave that more interesting company a gentle shoulder-pat of appreciation. *And something more?*

As the hallway group joined the sitting room group, Sara commanded Lois's attention: "I can explain away two sets of fingerprints. As you must know, Clara and I are well-known writers (Clara smiled her agreement) and we're always researching backgrounds for our mysteries. So we just looked into the Emerson suite. The door seemed to be opened and . . ."

"Don't play cat and mouse with me," said Lois completely unaware that a cat was a featured player in Clara and Sara's mysteries. She was just giving voice to her subconscious perception that Clara's smile made her look a bit like the Cheshire Cat.

"Well, we might have pushed the door a tad. Of course, our finger prints would be on it."

"You might find our fingerprints on a few of the other doors, too, even the Longfellow Room. That's the room that is, was, Marian's room," she stuttered, after a brief look asking for permission from Sara. "Some of the writers here have closed minds. They even have closed doors. So our fingerprints could possibly be found around some locks."

"All in the good cause of our literary research," Sara concluded for her.

"I want you to know" Officer Lois said, ignoring Sara and addressing the group, "although Nikki and Malcolm are guilty of a lot, they are not guilty of murder."

One of the other officers could be heard saying in an aside to a uniformed rookie, "No, the little perverts took videos of themselves during the night of the murder. Wow. They are . . ."

Lois gave him a look that stopped him mid-sentence. "I wouldn't put it that way, but we do know from dated video clips that Nikki and Malcolm Haverford were otherwise occupied during the period that the murder could have taken place. The official explanation is that Marian Rogers' death was due to a systemic collapse caused by a toxic substance, at this time unknown, and administered by a person or persons, also unknown at this time.

"Didn't you people notice that strange smile on the deceased's face? That is, you people who saw her dead. The medical term is *Risus Sardonicus*."

"Are you telling us something with that term, Detective, or trying to obscure some information from us?" asked Hans, knowing full well that what Lois was doing was enjoying the opportunity to show off her specialized knowledge.

"We police don't play with words the way you do. We use precise and technically accurate terms. *Risus Sardonicus* is a sustained contraction of facial muscles resulting in the somewhat sardonic smile you saw on Marian's face. It's a result of nervous system involvement, as in strychnine poisoning, which, by the way, we've already ruled out.

"We suspect that whoever broke into the Haverfords' apartment was looking for evidence, evidence that could be used against him or her, 'the person or persons unknown,' the possible perpetrators of the murder. Videotapes were taken from the Haverfords' Emerson Suite. The perps must have been pretty disappointed to find that they were useless. We had confiscated all of the tapes of anyone entering or leaving Marian's room any where near the crime time. We're a small police force in a small town, but even we know enough not to leave evidence lying around.

"Whoever the perps are, they goofed—more than once," she added. This closing ambiguous remark left everyone wondering, a device Lois had found effective in previous investigations, though Buck's comments about the three crimes wasn't exactly what she had expected: "It's going to be like fighting a pig in the mud to get this all straightened out."

audrey lavin

Chapter Seventeen

Thursday, continued

Tony's reaction was different, but so was Tony. "Mary Babe, I said it yesterday and I'm saying it again, I've gotta get out of here. I've gotta get you out of here, too. I'm going for a bike ride. I'm not going to ride a century, just explore for an hour or so."

In answer to Mary Beth's blank look, he explained, "Bikers have their talk just like you English Department types do. You talk about symbolism and simile; we talk about riding a century. That's going 100 miles, get it?

"Mary Babe, you go do your thing now. I'll pick you up later. I've got just the place we can escape to."

Ignoring the often-present tease in Tony's voice, Mary Beth thought, *What is this with the men in my life wanting to escape with me?*

She said, "Sure, Tony."

"Your car. My map, 'Highways and Byways of Ohio.' Not an evening at the *Maul*." He made a few hand gestures toward her body by way of explanation. " A real surprise. I promise."

Mary Beth's nod combined acknowledgment of Tony's pun with her agreement to his plan.

With that, Tony put on his Oakley M Frames, Lance Armstrong edition, of course, and temporarily disappeared outdoors. He was soon seen on his black Cannondale slowly circling the house at about ten miles per hour. Not in his most adult mode, he was laughing and furiously waving his bandana to all viewers who hurriedly pretended to be disinterested.

Mary Beth disappeared into her room and the obscure connections she was having fun establishing between Henry James and E. M. Forster.

On his way upstairs, Buck called loudly, "Anyone going to rustle up some grub for us today?"

Cook appeared, openly showing hostility. "Do you want dinner tonight?"

"What are my choices?"

"Yes or no."

An affirmative grunt demonstrated that Buck was more interested in getting food than in saving face—or his life? *Everyone was acting suspicious*, he thought. *Cook certainly was.* Continuing up the staircase to his studio, he resolved to be more respectful to Cook. *With what's going on in this house, I don't think I should be on the bad side of someone who prepares my food. My God, she uses herbs from her own uninspected herb garden, too."*

Hans sat chatting with Sara and Clara. "She was really a wonderful woman." He didn't feel it necessary to explain who he was talking about. Sara and Clara knew. "Beautiful, you could see, and so eloquent about life."

"I'd say she's eloquent about death, too," Sara replied.

"What do you mean?"

"A still body can often speak more clearly than an active one."

"What are you saying?"

"Look at that pose we found her in. That corpse is telling plenty to the right 'listener.' "

Without realizing it, Hans and Clara leaned toward Sara.

"Look at all of the research we've done for our books, Clare. No one's ever died that perfectly made-up. The killer or someone came into that room. Someone sat her up and fixed her up after she was dead. I'm sure."

Preoccupied with this somewhat ghoulish thought, the three writer-sleuths drifted off to their rooms where each of them more or less hid out for the rest of the working day.

The custom horn on Tony's bicycle disturbed them and other writers, thinkers, munchers and nappers around 5 o'clock. Mary Beth, in her good-girl way, had already filled out the official form for them to leave town for the evening and was sitting at the bar waiting for Tony. She rushed out to meet him before his noise became her responsibility.

Tony had folded himself into in the driver's seat of her P.T. Cruiser. "I'll drive," he informed her, and added, "I hope you had a good pre-cocktail hour snack at the bar. The dinner I promised you is going to be hot dogs and popcorn."

"Some surprise. Your menu is a dead give-away. We must be going to the ball game."

"Come on, Mary Babe. You know me better than that. I'll give you a hint. The popcorn we'll be eating will be made in a 1962 popcorn popper!"

They headed north. Was it Northeast? Northwest? Mary Beth didn't care about direction or popcorn poppers or, for a short time, about Marian. It was good to be driving again in an open car on an open road. Summer in Ohio with warm days and slightly cooler evenings is as perfect as it can be. But Tony wouldn't let the inhabitants of Prince George House stay far behind them.

"Your friend Hans is some dresser."

Mary Beth tried to laugh off what she perceived as Tony's competitive opening. "Oh, Tony, I'll bet he doesn't have as many black jeans as you do."

"Yeah. He has more suits than they do at the Men's Wearhouse. And I guarantee it."

Mary Beth didn't take the bait. Tony tried again. "That Buck's something else, too. He told me that the time he spent with the recently deceased, with Marian, were the best years of *her* life."

"Tony, leave my new friends alone. You'll see. In a few days, you'll get to like them as much as I do, though I'll admit Buck can be a little off-putting. But right now, I'm with you, Babe."

Tony smiled and concentrated on his driving. Mary Beth concentrated on Tony's new jealousy *or jealousies*, she corrected herself. After about an hour, the open landscape had disappeared. They were on the main street of a typical Ohio town, seeing tidy white frame house after white frame house built against the street. They passed the town's only three restaurants, each one rejecting its past and moving into the 21st century by proudly announcing that it specialized in Mexican food. Tony suddenly stepped on the brake and pulled up at a huge billboard, "Star Light Drive In."

"All this way to go to a drive-in for supper?"

"No. No, Mary-Babe. Look, girl, look." He gave her head a little push so that she now faced the smaller sign, "Drive In Movie Theater."

"Tony, how did you ever find this? I've heard of drive-ins, but never seen one. Didn't know they still existed."

"You ought to study your Ohio history more. Ohio leads the country with its thirty-six drive-in movie theaters. It's not just film buffs and nostalgia seekers like me who keep them going. They're still a bargain for families looking for a cheap evening out. Of course when the Star Light was built, Ohio had 196. That was about fifty years ago and the Star Light has been showing movies regularly since then. In 1956 it took twenty-four days to put it up at a cost of $100,000, which was real money back then."

"Tony, I'm a teacher. It's 'real money' to me right now."

Tony steered the car over to the ticket booth. They paid for their two tickets. "Hiding anyone under that blanket in back?" the attendant asked. Mary Beth and Tony laughed politely. "Believe me, it happens," she called out as they followed the gravel path to acres of parking spaces in front of what looked like acres of screen.

The acres of parking were clearly marked off into 500 spaces, evenly divided between the Star Light's widely separated screens. The screens were strategically placed and slightly tilted so that passengers in every car would have an excellent view of the screen. Next to each space was a speaker attached to an orange pole. Tony put their speaker in the car.

"Even though," he explained, "you can hear on the car stereo. This is more authentic."

"See how they even out the house, Mary Beth? The attendant directs the cars to clusters of unconnected parking areas, so if it's only half a house, like tonight, it looks full."

"Now for dinner, Mary-best. I told you, this is a real date." He proved it by coming around to her side of the car and opening the door for her with a flourish. Mary Beth instantly flashed back to a day ago when Hans had made the same gesture. She pulled herself back to the present, following Tony's playful manner by dramatically extending her hand. She tripped a little, but wasn't hurt when she landed on the clover based, grassy field.

Tony helped her get up, then grandly escorted her, past some youngsters playing Frisbee, to a grey cement block rectangular building. Inside of the basic structure were two projection booths (the theater was an early multiplex), the promised 1962 popcorn popper, a hot dog machine, and a well-pierced, sweet young thing behind the counter, who was dispensing orange pop and root beer. "Name your poison," she said. Mary Beth gasped and pointed to the orange.

Then, as Ohioans frequently do, Tony started a conversation with the man behind them in line. He turned out to be Rick, the owner manager, a man who liked his own hot dogs as well as his own movies. "We should have guessed he was the manager," Tony later told Mary Beth. "He was wearing a 'Star Light Drive In' T- shirt. Who else would?" Rick also sported an arty beard and aviator glasses that complimented his Birkenstocks. Running a drive-in was a way of life for him. In fact, they learned he was the third generation in this free-wheeling family business.

"We're all family," Rick added. "Big Jim here," pointing to Jim-here, "used to be a customer. He started helping me after a fight one night; now he's my assistant and official bouncer.

"C'mon and see the projectors," he said between his and their mouthfuls. Tony couldn't wait. He'd read in one of his engineering journals that the Starlight boasted a 1940s projector. *What a treat*. Rick explained that the films were shipped from Hollywood on twenty-minute reels. "We show first-run films from the first weekend of April until the end of October. But tonight, I suppose you're here for our once a season 'Classic Crime Retrospective?'"

"Oh, Tony, how great!"

"That's part of the surprise, Mary Beth."

"Tonight's cult classics are *The Mirror Crack'd from Side to Side* and Frank Capra's *Arsenic and Old Lace*. *The Mirror* is the 1980 version of Agatha Christie's book with Angela Lansbury as that know-it-all Miss Marple. She's not quite as good as Joan Hickson, Christie's first choice, but she plays a more than adequate lady detective. You'll enjoy it."

"I'd love to see them both, but let's leave at intermission, Tony. We've seen that 1944 *Arsenic and Old Lace* on TV recently. It is a riot. As the ads for it say, 'Madness gallops through it!' But I'm determined to get a good night's sleep. I've got that work-in-progress that I really have to nudge along."

"O.K., hon, though I'm sure your WIP-meter is running just fine."

"Either way, we're glad to have you here," Rick said. "We're always glad to see new faces. We get a lot of regulars, like Duke, here, who comes every Saturday and the McAllen family who come every Sunday, aficionados you'd call them. They have their preferred parking spots, too."

"Just like students in my classes," Mary Beth pointed out.

"Yep. Duke parks over at the right side of the concession stand every time. He comes early to get *his* space. Toby and Tammy are always in the third row from the front. The regulars come early to get their favorite spaces.

"We get mainly families in mini-vans and a lot of young couples who come here to create their own families."

In answer to Mary Beth's questioning look, he added, "People who come to see the movie, usually head for the first three rows. People who have other occupations on their mind park waaay in the back.

"Show time. Have a nice evening."

"Have you noticed, Mary Babe, that around here people say 'Have a nice evening' or 'Have a good day' as if they really mean it."

"This is Ohio, Tony. They do."

The projectors started and Mary Beth and Tony headed back to their car for an enjoyable evening watching an old flick under the stars, pretending to live in the even older world of the film. Even though the story takes place in the manor house of a "typical" English village in the "innocent"-50s, Mary Beth was quick to point out that all of the murder suspects were American. And what a cast. Mary Beth and Tony were constantly nudging each other as a generation of famous stars were paraded across the screen by director Guy Hamilton: Elizabeth Taylor, Rock Hudson, Tony Curtis, Geraldine Chaplin, Kim Novak, and even a very young Pierce Brosnan added to the fun.

"That over-the-top acting of every cast member was a little much," Tony commented as he backed the car out of their assigned parking space while credits were still rolling.

"I know. It's odd being paired with *Arsenic*. That's full of over-the-top acting, too. But in *Arsenic*, Cary Grant, Josephine Hull, Peter Lorre, Raymond Massey, and Edward Everett Horton make it work. I wonder how it would have turned out if Ronald Reagan had taken the Cary Grant role of Mortimer Brewster. He was offered it first, y'know. I'm glad I'm not a director."

On the quiet way home, Mary Beth and Tony's awareness of their own in-house murder was heightened by the cumulative effect of seeing Miss Marple solve a murder and thinking of the two nice Victorian lady murderers they had skipped.

"Mary-Best, did you have to memorize 'The Lady of Shallot' when you were in high school? I sure did! I don't recall most of it. I think she was watching Camelot in the mirror; then something like, 'The mirror crack'd from side to side/the curse is come upon me/cried the Lady of Shalott.' It's like you. Your writing group at Prince George House is Camelot (Mary Beth snickered) and when Marian died and Nikki and Malcolm were arrested, that mirror you were watching it all in, that mirror cracked from side to side and a few other places too."

"Tony-hon, you should have been an English teacher instead of an engineer."

"We all think in metaphors, Mary-Best, even engineers."

Chapter Eighteen

Thursday night

While Mary Beth and Tony were watching fictional crimes being solved by unlikely fictional detectives, Lois was listening to new evidence about the all too real murder of Marian Roberts.

Ernie, the police department's white-hat hacker, had completed his assignment of examining all of the computers at Prince George House. Wired and wiry, Ernie usually looked as if he were ready to pounce, belying his patience and ability to spend hours working out any computer problem.

He had been typically thorough and ethical as befitted his white-hat title. All machines had been quarantined. All plugs had been pulled. He removed the hard drives and secured each one in his Disc Jockey Forensic Kit, a necessary legal protection. He knew that the Lakeville Prosecutor's Office wouldn't want to give any defense lawyer the opportunity to say that the police or prosecutors had distorted the evidence by writing on a disc after the fact.

When he tagged the files that had any bearings on motive or crime, he had taken time to sort and categorize the data, recording drive contents and the date and time stamp where relevant.

On Thursday afternoon, Ernie had printed out all of the pertinent material he had so carefully organized and presented Lois with a file full of hard copies to digest and, he hoped, to use in finding the culprits. In his hack mode, Ernie was a creative trouble-shooter who was so focused that he was almost unreachable. Lois had been impatient for the results she was now holding in her hand. She was familiar with the "Google Murder" and similar cases. Some of the evidence that convicted the killer in the Google murder case was found in the Google search the suspect carried out the day before the killing. Among other topics, he researched "tips with killing with a baseball bat" (the weapon used) and "how to murder someone and not get caught." Ernie's information could potentially break the case.

Afternoon had transitioned into evening. This was the time of day when most normal people who had a life were out enjoying themselves. But not Lois and Ernie. They were two of a kind, two who were on the happy verge of being workaholics.

Lois was ready to discuss the information contained in the files. Ernie sat across the desk from her waiting for the approval he knew he deserved. Lois was computer literate enough to be aware of her limits and to know that Ernie with his programming and technical skills was megahertzes (*or something like that,* she thought) ahead of her.

"Good job, Ernie. I haven't read everything, but we have plenty of information here to convict Nikki and Malcolm of voyeurism, identity theft, and related crimes. Unfortunately for us, their films and computer continue to display plenty of evidence that exonerates them from the more serious crime of Marian's murder.

"Let's go through the materials you've downloaded from the other computers."

"It's not a lot, Lois, even though I checked out transportable media, too. But that drew a blank. No one did anything like disguising secret files as their music CD's.

"Tony didn't even bring a computer with him, so there were just the four PC's to examine, the ones 'Ohio Creates' supplied to Mary Beth, Sara and Clara, Hans, and Buck. And remember, they've only had the computers for a few days. Granted, Hans and Buck also brought laptops which have more info on them. I'll tell ya' they're some odd group; they've all made ID-Ten-T errors about poisons."

"What do you mean?"

"I'll let you in on a little computer talk, Lois. ID-Ten-T. Write it out."

"Ah, ha. I.D.10.T. ID10T."

"Yeah, they're all ID-Ten-Ts. Each one of these writers has looked up a website related to poison at some time this week. You can see that each file I've flagged has the time and date stamped on it. They're almost all before the murder. I was able to retrieve all of that information even though recently some of these writers realized the potentially incriminating effect poison searches would have. They've tried to eliminate complete files or just the dates."

"Even if I don't talk the talk, I agree, Ernie—these guys are odd. The question is, what makes them odd. Malice? Curiosity? Or do some of them have other valid reasons for looking up poisons? Let's start with the two laptops."

"O.K. Hans and Buck are the ones with the laptops. We'll take them one at a time, but you should know that they do use them the same way. Their professional work, such as it is, is on the PC; their personal notes or e-mail are on the laptops. But here they diverge."

"Me, too, Lois. Speaking of laptops, did you ever hear the one about the two fonts who walked into a bar?" He hurried on before she could stop him. "The bartender said 'Get out we don't want your type here.' Get it? 'Your type?' " He chuckled.

"Ernie, what is the matter with you? What are you stalling about? Let's get down to business."

"I guess that was a rather crude stall. It's because I don't think you've had time to look at all of the print-outs yet. Buck's laptop is full of a lot of embarrassing and lurid wish fulfillment."

"So?"

"Well, you're the object of that wish fulfillment."

Lois' coloring approximated the color of her hair. Ernie's was close.

"Let's stick to what's relevant to the crime."

"Neither of their laptops seems to have anything even slightly related to the crime. Buck did check out one website that I thought might be a lead, 'Cowboys and Poisons,' but it proved to be meaningless. Most of his web-searches are on his PC. I'll get to that in a minute. His laptop is full of you plus lists of jokes that he is changing into cowboy jokes. Like, did you hear the one about the rather small cowboy sitting at a bar nursing his drink?"

"Ernie!"

"Yes ma'am. Hans has opened up the 'Police Notebook' site a few times and he's put serious study hours into identity theft. I'm only surprised that more of the writers haven't checked out identity and intellectual property after the way they all were used by Nikki and Malcolm. Hans' laptop is full of e-mails to and from his agent. They all seem to be related to his not getting his work in on time. The agent is unhappy about his lack of progress. I'll tell ya', Lois, who knows what progress is with that kind of writing?"

"I agree, but save the editorial comments. What about the desk computers or whatever you call them?"

"Like I said, all of those guys were checking poison sites. It looks like Sara and Clara knew a lot about poison plants. Except their interest was limited to what they found on 'Plant Smarts'. They were, and I kid you not, trying to rhyme poisons."

"Oh," Lois explained, "that's how they do the titles of their books."

"They weren't having much success then. I'll read you a few of their rhyming attempts. You'll get the idea. Quickly. Pardon the meter. It's theirs, not mine. 'Clara and Sara raid/ that deadly nightshade,' 'Clara and Sara find the foe/hidden away in mistletoe,' and what's bound to be the title of a best seller, 'Belladonna/ I'm Yo' Mama.' "

"That's enough, Ernie," Lois said, breaking out in laughter. "What else have we got?"

"We've got a lot of nothin'. But maybe you'll find something I missed. That teacher cum detective has an annotated list of all of the flowers in the Syberstone wild flower garden. It doesn't look suspicious. Notes are like, 'Spring Beauty and Toothwort still blooming.' Pretty innocent sounding to me, but she also checked on sites like, 'poisons in your garden.' She's even got half an article written proving that maybe the reason everyone is so mixed up in *The Turn of the Screw* is that they've been nibbling on some hallucinatory wild flowers. The problem is she can't figure out which plant it could be. She's got sentences where cannabis is the culprit, some where peyote cacti is the bad guy, even salvia divinorum. Hey, I cook with sage all the time.

"If you'll look through that file, you'll find a copy of an e-mail she sent to herself. 'Check with Gordon in Biology: If people get high on wild moonseed in Ohio, what's the related species that does the same thing in England?' "

"That still sounds like she's working on one of her crack-pot literary theories. What about the men? Anything in Hans' or Buck's computers?"

"As I said, Hans is having writing problems. What do I know? Maybe that's the way he creates. He has some other problem, too. He's fighting with some tech in the Philippines in a peculiar e-mail conversation. But mainly he has pages of lists and lists. Like a list of famous poisoners, then the sentence, 'The only good book is a finished book,' then a list of famous cases, followed by almost the same sentence, 'The best book is a finished book.' If I had to guess, I'd say he's searching for ideas. But you don't like guesses do you, Lois?"

"Instinct has its place in detective work, Ernie. You've searched a lot of computers. I'd give weight to what you call your 'guesses' and I'd call 'a knowledgeable reorganization of known facts.' And Buck?"

"Buck is the only one who really seems to be writing. I might as well warn you again, Lois, that his heroine, that lusty, busty Rusty, has more than a passing resemblance to you. He's been researching poisoned drinks that she seems to dispense with ease. One thing I know is that this guy Buck is not what he seems. I've heard people talk about his kind of dumb cowpoke role, but the sites he looked up are a few steps ahead of that bowlegged curve. '*Liber herbarum*' is all in German. You might want to get a translator. Another one is 'Shakespeare's Sonnets.' Some of the sites really had recipes for poisoned drinks, like a poisoned peach martini. The recipe I like is for poison water made up of 7 Up, vodka and clear rum. The site says 'Try it, you'll see why it's called poison water.' Which reminds me, Lois, I could finish up this evening with something to drink. How about you?"

"Let's keep it professional, Ernie. Keep in mind, I'm almost twice your age."

"That's the new tadpoling, Lois. Stop thinking so much. Just go with it. The guy or tadpole is supposed to be half the woman's age, then it's either plus or minus seven years, but what do we care. I'm talking about a drink, not a life-time commitment."

But Lois couldn't stop thinking. She considered all possibilities, all implications. It was her university police training.

"You know, Ernie, I have a friend."

"Lois, you're an intelligent woman. Do me a favor, weigh an Ernest against a Jon André."

Lois burst out laughing. "But this is not winner take all," she said as she walked out of the door with Ernie.

Chapter Nineteen

Thursday night, continued, and Friday morning

Mary Beth had been busy thinking, too. In fact, she had been unusually quiet most of the way during the drive back to Lakeville. Somehow "The Mirrror Crack'd" made her think of E. M. Forster and Henry James again. *What didn't?* she asked herself. It was the flick's not differentiating very much between British English and American English that did it. Mary Beth remembered that Forster had accused James of a similar flaw, that of having all of his characters in *The Ambassadors* speak the same language whether they are French or English. Mary Beth couldn't remember the quote exactly, but she knew where to look it up. She was sure that in *Angels,* Forster stressed the difference between Italian and English. He said something like, "Italian is a bad medium for condescension. The patronizing words come out gracious and sincere." She'd find that and a few other citations showing that Forster, but not James, was aware that different languages expressed different social realities.

"Ouch, Tony." The pothole he hit jarred the car and her thinking. She could hardly wait to get back to her solid desk to work on her study.

On entering Prince George House again, she immediately distanced herself from Tony. She had decisions to make by herself: What she planned to do about her work-in-progress, her romances-in-progress, the crimes that had been in-progress during the past few days. Partly she wanted to be in bed with . . . *with whom*? She definitely needed some quiet time, some time to think.

Tony needed some private time as well. "I still have some papers to work on tonight, Mary-Best, diagrams to finish. They'll help me explain things to you. First, you have to understand, 'Without geometry, life is pointless.' That awful quote is from my math professor. He used to tell me to work harder, that a base in solid geometry would come in handy some day. Even he'd be surprised at how handy! I'm going to take you on a really unusual house tour tomorrow morning."

"Tony, after a week like this, I don't need any more 'unusual.' How about if I opt out and spend some time with James and Forster and my WIP?"

"If that's a question, the answer is a big 'NO, Mary-Babe. We can't do less; we have to do more. I want to ratchet this investigation up a little."

"Don't you need to be away from all of this some more? That trip back in time to the drive-in was perfect. We were lucky that the rain held off. Listen, it's just beginning now. I'm getting so I can't even think with all of this going on. I'm going to retreat into my studio for the night."

"Is that an invitation, Mary Babe?" Tony could see from her face that it wasn't! He tried to cover the fact that he sometimes misunderstood her. "I work in a bike shop, Mary Best, in what you English Department types would call an interruption rich environment. People are always rushing in with 'fix this' or 'adjust that.' All of these people here and their problems actually help me think."

"I guess there would be a certain synergy, Tony. But I can't believe that people whose peculiarities I've grown fond of in just a couple of days have been murdered and have been arrested. I must be a lousy judge of character."

"Instead of berating yourself, Mary Best, come over to the dark side."
"What?"
"Pretend you're a murderer. What would you do? Where would you do it? Why would you dress Marian up? She was inert; it would be like dressing a doll."

"How gruesome, Tony. Couldn't you have just ended this lovely evening with, 'Pleasant dreams' "?

The light rain that started Thursday night had turned into a downpour in the predawn hours of Friday. It's drumming of a double paradiddle on the roof and driveway awoke most of the writers on Friday morning. Mary Beth turned in her bed and found herself alone. *Who do I wish was here?* was the first question she asked herself again that morning. It was quickly followed by her self-critical refrain, *The older I get, the more sluttish I get*. She changed tack and tried to recapture her dream. Something important had been in it. It had been about Turkey. The increasing rain must have reminded her of her first few days in Izmir when the rains were so heavy that the streets were flooded, as were the entrance and exits to the hotel she had been staying in.

In her dream, as in Izmir, when Mary Beth put on all of her rain gear and went outside, it was to see Izmirites (?) Izmirians(?), she never did learn the correct term, constructing makeshift and humorously unreliable bridges across the flooded streets. They used large storage containers, plastic baskets, metal and plastic trash cans—none of which was successful. Water was knee deep and rising. Everyone was soaked. Men in business suits or jeans, women in slacks or chadors. Every so often a temporary "bridge" would hold for a while, then float away, leaving someone literally up a creek. Schools and businesses were closed. A holiday "we're all in this together" atmosphere had prevailed.

Mary Beth had no trouble piecing together that part of her dream, but something else happened that she struggled to recapture. *Just before I woke up, some thing happened, something that had to do with Prince George House, something I need to remember. Maybe a cup of tea will help.*

The percussion level of the rainstorm had abated by the time Mary Beth exited her room. She saw Sara tip-toeing out of hers. Had Mary Beth caught her in the middle of a nefarious scheme? No, Sara was trying to give Clara an extra hour's sleep. Mary Beth had to remind herself that every action at Prince George wasn't menacing.

The two women started down the stairs at the same time with the same thoughts in their minds: breakfast and murder. On the way to the dining room, Mary Beth told Clara about the movie she and Tony had seen and the one they had not seen the previous evening. *"The Mirror Cracked* had three murders; they were all by poison put in drinks."

"You can add thirteen more to that list, Mary Beth. Those sweet little old ladies in *Arsenic and Old Lace* murdered thirteen men, and all of them were by poison in beverages, too."

"Gives one pause, doesn't it, Clara?"

Back at the station house, Officer Lois sat in her office surrounded by trash bags filled with carefully identified refuse. Each room of Prince George House was represented from the first floor powder room to Tony's recently put into use bedroom. Lois put on her latex gloves and tackled what was in all respects a dirty job, the careful examination of each bag. In preparation she had adjusted her computer and head set. The attached microphone was ready. She would carefully record the garbage search as she had recorded all details of the police investigation. Later she would type up and transmit the notes to her murder log. Lois turned her swivel chair toward the largest bag and began to itemize objects of interest from Monday's sweepings and deposits while she grumbled.

"Why me?

"Kitchen garbage from day after murder," she announced. This was followed by various "ughs" escaping from Lois into the permanent record. She went on listing, "Some unknown foodstuffs, paper goods, plastic wrap, rubber gloves, crumbled foil, potato parings, everything you'd expect to find in kitchen trash—except—" Even though she was wearing gloves, she used tongs to lift up some soiled book covers. She read the title and description into the mic: *"Billy Blue* by the author of *Gracie Green* and *Rachel Red.* The hard, glossy cover and back of a children's book with interior pages missing, in fact, cut out. Cover is ideal for holding latent prints. Might be unrelated to crime, but so far, the only item I had not expected to find in materials taken from kitchen rubbish can."

Lois continued to investigate, swiveling to the smaller bags of more personal junk collected from the waste baskets emptied from each bedroom. By now she had forgotten she was wired and accompanied her search with many a "Why me?" and "Ugh. Ugh." Until finally a "Eureka!" Unfolding page after page of authors' discarded, not-so-promising manuscripts had paid off. Here in the plastic sack labeled, "Library" were many of the pages that had been cut from *Billy Blue*. Once she ascertained that the pages themselves had a light blue cast, she had no problem re-assembling the book. *Is Gracie Green on green stock and Rosie Red on red? I suppose so,* she thought as she fished the pages out of the collected trash and put them in numerical order, noting which pages were missing. *Being an investigator, I'll investigate. But everyone has access to that library. Would any of those writers be so bored that they'd notice someone throwing away papers? We'll have to ask later.*

Some pages were still missing. Lois kept on searching through the plastic bags of refuse, now with the energy brought on by having a definite purpose. And she was rewarded. The missing pages turned up in the contents of the waste basket from the Henry James room. *That's Mary Beth's room. Who had access to her room and the library? Mary Beth. And Tony? But he wasn't here when Marian was murdered. Was he?*

The test for fingerprints was swift and efficient. Two different sets of prints were found. The thumb on the glossy front cover and three fingers on the back were an easy match to Mary Beth's. Lois decided to make a second trip to Prince George House to confront her.

But first, this was the third Friday of June. Even in the middle of a murder, detective Lois wouldn't miss her monthly Lois Club luncheon. A few hours later, she was glad she had been at the meeting. One result of the brief resurgence of Lois as a popular name in the '70's was some younger members joining the Lakeville chapter. So that, amidst all of the grandchild and new baby comparisons, Lois had, or was handed, an idea. In a discussion about generational differences, some of the younger women gave examples of their mother's quaint habit of wearing aprons and rubber gloves. *Does Cook wear gloves?* wondered Lois. *I*

just took it for granted that the ones I found in the kitchen trash were
hers. But maybe someone wanted me to think that. I'll check the gloves
out tomorrow. I have to go over to Prince George House now.

She was still curious to hear Mary Beth's explanation of the prints
on the book cover. She'd get to the gloves and the pages found in her
waste basket later.

Lois's personal style was down-home, but in her way, she was as
skilled as Nikki or Marian at making an entrance. When she arrived at
the house mid-morning and entered the library with her all-business-all-
the-time stride, she commanded the situation. All eyes turned towards
her. She turned her eyes toward Mary Beth saying, "Let's step into the
entrance hall for a few minutes." Lois's questions followed immediately.

Mary Beth, while trying to be polite, was angry and defensive at
seriously being considered connected with the crime. "Although being
a suspect, Officer, gives me a somewhat contrived sensation of living
dangerously, I don't. I'm just an English Professor trying to write an
article. There's a pretty simple reason for my prints being on the book's
cover." Mary Beth then explained to Lois how the book had been
delivered to her for review at the opening meet- and-greet party, and
how she had passed it on to Marian.

It wasn't surprising then that the slightly smudged right index print
at the corner of almost every page matched the one taken from Marian's
cadaver. Lois had already sent it to State for confirmation of her theory
that Marian was one of those finger-lickin' page turners, and that the
poison could have been delivered that way if someone else shared her
knowledge.

Clara walked in during Mary Beth's explanation and refused to
notice that Lois, who didn't want to stop the flow of conversation, was
giving her hand signals to get out.

"Are you talking about that kiddie lit book?"

"What kiddie lit book?" Lois asked, suspicious of the jargon.

"The kiddie lit book mailed to you, Mary Beth, the one you gave
Marian to read or work on. I don't want to hurt your feelings," she
smiled too sweetly. *What does that mean? "* But I called the book editor

of the *Inquirer*. He's an old friend of the movie-balcony sort, if you know what I mean. Though you probably think I'm too old to have relationships."

Mary Beth squirmed. Of course, that's what she thought.

"He says they never sent a book to you. They don't get reviewers cold, that way. And furthermore, here's the clincher, my dear, he's never heard of you. Not ever."

"Somebody sent me that book."

"Yes, somebody who knew you'd pass it on to Marian. I think that's the missing piece to the puzzle. Of course, it could be the missing piece to an entirely different puzzle. But we won't know until we find it."

Buck strode up to them then. "I overheard you talking about that book. You're right. It's got to be important. So important that I'll take the reins here."

Mary Beth and Clara gave each other looks they meant Buck to see. And he did. "My bad again," he said and went for more coffee.

With little effort Officer Lois had been able to keep her disinterested poker face during this exchange. She was bored with the writers' shenanigans and in-fighting and felt that the only true professional around. She certainly wasn't going to discuss her finds with the likes of them until she was ready.

Lois studied each of the writers as they spoke. She knew that creating a complex plot was second nature to each of them. That's what they did. What she would do was to return to her source of clues (*Yes, ugh, back to the trash,* she reminded herself) to continue her investigation. But first she thought she should stir things up a bit and remind them who she was.

"Mary Beth," she asked, "do you think anyone from Midfield Campus College could have been responsible for sending that book? I know you have some weirdos on your faculty at McCollege."

Mary Beth's response was a startled. "How do you know where I teach?"

Lois turned to leave, first saying (a tad smugly), "I'm the police, you know."

audrey lavin

Chapter Twenty

Friday morning

Mary Beth and Tony sought refuge with each other. They huddled together at the far end of the dining room. "What's next, Mary Beth? I guess we should do what good detectives always do, follow the money. *Cui bono*? Who benefits from Marian's death?"

"That won't help. Buck, who seems to know a surprising amount about Marian's will, told someone that she left all of her money to a children's literacy group, a real paradox if you know Marian's attitude toward hard cash."

"Paradox? I thought that meant two physicians."

Mary Beth grimaced. "Actually, Tony, Marian's leaving her money to children's literacy is fitting. And will be profitable, too. They'll buy her books. The money will go to the estate. And the estate will pay it back out to children's literacy. But it sure puts a stop to that line of questioning."

"We could have individual meetings with the other authors, Tony, to see if we can pick up any clues. We did that once before when Les was killed at Midfield. Remember?"

"Yes, but did it really help?"

"Help or not, I think that's the only thing left for us to do. But how can we when Hans is supposed to be on our team? That means we would be interviewing three on one. Two on one is bad enough, but three on one would be counterproductive."

"O.K, Mary Beth, let's interview Hans first. He's as much a suspect as anyone. I've been wondering about him since the get go."

"What? Just because he's my, my what? My special friend?" Mary Beth had the decency to blush at her use of the word "friend."

"Maybe a little because he's your so 'special friend,' but mainly because everyone, except for the two of us, is suspect. We'll interview him and if that goes well, discuss our plan. I'm sure he'll be glad to let us interview the others. He's a little too aesthetic and intellectual to push hard questions. Let's just say we want to talk over our crime solving methodology with him."

By then all attempts to maintain the original work and meal schedule for "Ohio Creates" had disappeared. Hans was downstairs imbibing a late breakfast. He was stirring his coffee as if he were a connoisseur, which, in fact he was. But his purpose had less to do with coffee aroma than it had to do with his quietly studying the huddle involving Mary Beth and Tony. He was pleased when that broke up and they walked over to him. He tried to start a conventional conversation: "Cook has put out an excellent breakfast," he said, "though, under the circumstances, I wouldn't try her herbal tea."

"You're right," Tony agreed. "I hear Cook is an arbitrator."

"What?"

"Yes, she left a job at Arby's to come to work for Nikki and Malcolm. Arby-traitor, get it?"

"Tony-y-y," Mary Beth groaned.

Tony smiled at her and said, "Hans, let's go out to the garden to talk. We can take our coffee . . . and tea," he added, remembering Mary Beth's choice of breakfast beverages.

"And croissants," Hans filled out their menu, making unnecessarily long eye contact with Mary Beth, who startled her complacent self by reacting with a frisson of pleasure.

"And that wonderful Cooper's marmalade," Mary Beth continued filling up the final empty space on the breakfast tray Hans was carrying.

"Is that the Original Cooper's or is it Vintage Cooper's?" Hans asked.

"It certainly isn't the Fine-Cut," Mary Beth replied.

"So much to say; so little time to say it in," Tony muttered to himself.

The three concerned writers sat on the first stone bench in the garden. Mary Beth and Tony filled Hans in on Lois's morning call. They didn't have to start asking Hans questions.

"I can't figure this out," he said as soon as they stopped their explanation. "I was in the library with Buck. Then I went upstairs. My room is next to his. On the other side of the hall is Marian's room; that's directly across from Buck's. Then the girls; you know, Sara and Clara's; then yours, Mary Beth, aptly named the Henry James room. You are writing about James and Forster now, aren't you? I know you know all of this, but I'm going to make a little schema of the rooms; it'll help me think better." He took a paper napkin from the tray and, in a minute, presented Mary Beth and Tony with a simple diagram.

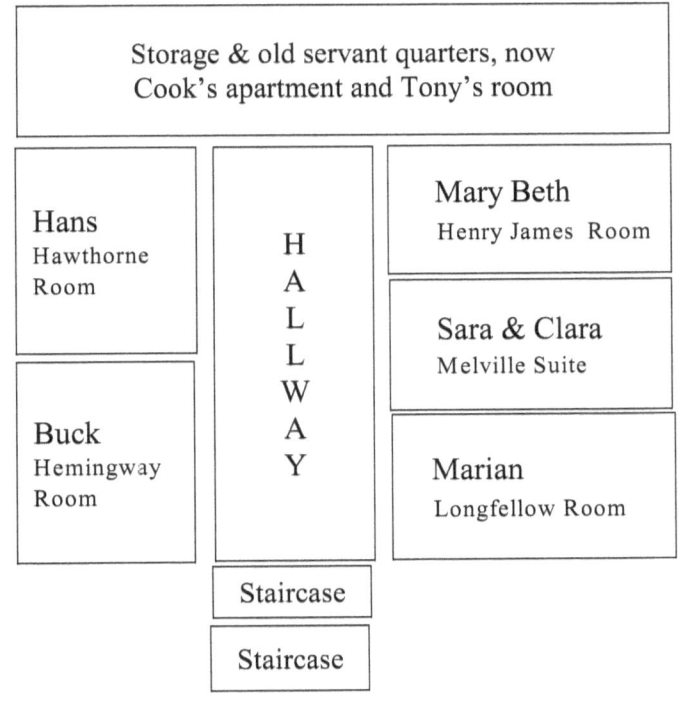

"It's pretty symmetrical. The staircase starts in the reception or entrance room and goes up through the middle of the house; Marian has. . . well, the room has a balcony. But I didn't hear a sound. Buck says he didn't either. I would have heard someone coming up those creaky stairs and going into Marian's room. And even these small town detectives have searched to see that no one came in through the balcony. Someone must have been already in the room or put poison in a drink or something like that. Each one of us had a reason to dislike her, but to murder her? That's something else."

"And your reason for 'dislike'?"

"She was a user. Did you see that movie *All About Eve*? Eve manipulates people so that she can take over the life and career of Margo Channing, played by Bette Davis. Marian was just as seductive and conniving. I have to admit that each one of the guys she used, used her too. But my use was simple: sex and arm candy. She was excellent at both."

"Never mind. We don't need full details. What did she use you for?"

"Oh, her upward mobility. I introduced her to my agent at a party. Within two weeks she had left hers far behind and was Brown and Sons' favorite client. She saw to it that she was the newest star in their firmament. The promotional budget was skewed to help her sales. Even though we wrote in different genres, she managed to push me down and out of the way. Out of her way, too, once she had what she wanted. So yes, I had reason to dislike her, but I'm civilized. I would have made that dislike felt, I hoped, in a professional way."

"Not that I had any trouble finding a new and more demanding agent," he found it necessary to quickly add.

"Mary Beth and I can't figure it out either, Hans. We thought we'd try to talk separately with each of the other writers. We can bring our reports back to you. Maybe in organizing and verbalizing our results for you, we'll bring forward some clues. What do you think?"

"Go ahead." Without realizing he was doing it, Hans possessively gripped Mary Beth's shoulder; his hand stayed there. Tony's eyes widened. Hans ignored the implicit signal and said, "I don't have any better ideas. The whole process is anathema to me. And I really want to get back to my work to get away from all of this for a while. I'm having some problems with my writing. And it's not just writers' cramp." He gave a knowing smile to Mary Beth and continued, "Could each one of us, could any one of us write any thing worth while in a week? Could we write something that would make sense out of our lives or could we even make an unknown reader. . . I digress." He moved his hand.

"Off the top of my head, the only suggestion I have is a negative one: don't interview Sara and Clara together. We too often treat them as a single entity. They aren't. I'll admit, I found them a little insipid when I first met them, but now I think they're quite sipid, especially Sara."

Hans abruptly got up from the bench and left as Tony grudgingly said, "Good point."

Somewhat surprised, Tony turned to Mary Beth, "Well, this is number one and the fun has just begun."

"Tony, be serious. We have a murder on our hands. We're quite possibly living with the murderer."

Still facing Mary Beth on the bench, Tony could see Sara whose determined stride was bringing her directly and rapidly to where they were sitting. Tony, ducking the impending conversation, just as determinedly and rapidly, got up. "This is number two and I'll leave her up to you."

"Tony-y-y." Now with Sara in front of her, Mary Beth turned her almost-wail into, "Tony, g'bye. See you later." She smiled a greeting at Sara, "I've wanted to talk with you. Let's walk around this exquisite garden. So much has happened, I haven't had a chance to appreciate how well the Syberlings laid it out," she babbled on, unsettled by Tony's leaving her alone as chief investigative officer.

"I know Mr. Syberling was famous for his interest in man's place in nature and how that could be expressed in his landscaping. In fact, I've been trying to identify the wildflowers in this jewel of a garden. They're all from Ohio. I know that because I went over to the Historical Society and got a list. I can recognize the large flowered Trilium and the common Buttercup, but I haven't a clue as to which ones are the Indian

Pipes or the Daisy Fleabanes. Fleabanes? for Pete's sake. I wonder if any of them are hallucinogenic."

Sara's response was unexpected, "Mary Beth, what are you rambling on about? Right now I don't care about this garden or any Ohio wildflowers. I want to talk with you and Tony or you alone or almost anyone. I can't take this. Our Sara and Clara mysteries are all logical. This isn't. It's a real murder and it's messy. It's horrible."

Sara reiterated her brief, edge of hysteria, monologue. Then again. She couldn't stop. She obviously felt compelled to relive aloud the experiences of the past few days and to explain what she thought had happened:

"Everyone here hated her, you know. She collected enemies the way I collect doggies. Yes, I have a secret vice. In our cat-filled world, I have a secret yen for little porcelain doggies. I have a room full of them. Even and especially Clara doesn't know about them. Now you do, so arrest me." Mary Beth assumed that somewhere in this almost-hysterical outpouring of love for "doggies" and hate for "her," Sara was talking about Marian. She decided not to interrupt Sara's flow of emotion to confirm this.

"She hung around at one of my book signings and made friends with me, told me I could write without Clara and better than Clara. It's true I can. But I need Clara and her cats for ideas and motivation. We click on plots people genuinely like. Marian lured me into writing on my own. The result is my only single author book, *Free. Free and Aghast.*

"Marian saw to it that everyone was— aghast, that is. She savagely evaluated my work in public, in a big article in the *New York Times Book Review*. I can see now that she tried to destroy me to get Clara to work with her. Mare and Clare, or something like that. She wanted to break into the lucrative world of adult murder mysteries. She felt her kiddie lit was getting her in a rut. Think about it, the only difference between a rut and a grave is the depth."

Mary Beth kept a straight face, but her mind was racing: *What is she saying? I wish Tony had stayed. Is she incriminating herself?*

"Once she had me separated from Clara, she told me and the world that my writing was irredeemably pathetic." Sara began to sob.

"Are you telling me that you had a reason to kill her?"

Sara replied with quickly mustered control, "No, I'm not. Don't be silly. You consistently underestimate me. You underestimate Clara too, though I'm certainly the brains of our team. Just because we're not cute and skinny. . ." She stopped and critically eyed Mary Beth's tight sweater, "Maybe you're not skinny. But you know what I mean. Clara and I act our age, except maybe around young men." Sara had the good grace to laugh at her weakness for Eric. "I'm not dumb enough to name myself 'suspect-in-chief.' I'm trying to tell you that everyone here had a reason to kill her. It wasn't that Marian was asking for trouble; she needed it. Somehow it fueled her. Even Malcolm had a motive, though seemingly, he's innocent . . . of that."

"What in the world do you mean?" Mary Beth asked.

"Marian wouldn't have made the first cut to be here. She was a good enough writer, but this is supposed to be a compatible group, editing and critiquing each others' works. Come on, would you want that witch critiquing your work? She only got here by blackmailing Malcolm."

Sara sat back on the bench, smugly expecting the incredulous, "What?" that greeted her statement.

Both of the women were too engrossed in their conversation to stop to greet Tony who had pulled up a wrought iron chair to the bench and joined them.

Sara recognized his presence by addressing her comments to him as well as to Mary Beth. "You're astonished to hear they had an on-going affair while he was illustrating her books? Everyone in the literary world knew. Everyone except Nikki. And he didn't want her to. So Marian got whatever she wanted out of him. This free week in Lakeville is nothing. She also had a guarantee of free illustrations for her next book. I'm sure Malcolm felt there would be a next book and a next book and a next book. Malcolm, with all of his faults, is a well-known, accomplished artist. He pulls in big bucks, but all he ever got from his commissions from Marian was a few credit lines. Her death freed him. Or would have freed him: society is going to put him away for a while for his own disgusting crimes."

"You've put me away for a while, Sara, at least my hubris. I had no idea any of this was going on. Did you, Tony?"

"Are you kidding? I've been repairing bikes back in Midfield. I thought you were having a peaceful week writing." He looked at Sara. He saw her now as more of a colleague than as an older, dumpy woman. "You've opened my eyes to a lot of stuff, Sara. Everyone does have a motive. That complicates the investigation just as much as if no one had a motive. It's hard to believe. Even Malcolm." Tony unfolded himself from the chair and stretched.

Mary Beth took the hint. "Thanks for your time, Sara," she said. She, too, was ready to bring the conversation to a close, eager to get away from what looked like a dead end and on to more investigating. "You should know that we'll be talking with Clara."

"Don't tell her you-know-what, Mary Beth," Sara pleaded. "If she knew about my darling doggies, I'd never hear the end of it."

She quickly changed tone, "What about that Carter. . . Buck as he calls himself? Have you questioned him? He's been kind to me, but I don't know what he's capable of doing. Sometimes I think he's not a very evolved man."

Chapter Twenty-one

Friday noon

"Mary Babe, whata ya' think? Should I take you on that house tour I promised you? Or should we talk with Clara next or Buck, Sara's not-very-evolved man?"

"Sara's right, you know, though who can tell what he hides behind the redneck cowboy mask he puts on most of the time?

"But to answer your question, Tony, let's go on your tour later. The house can wait; it's not going anyplace. For now, let's find Clara and talk with her before she and Sara get together and conjoin their stories."

"What stories? We didn't even think about asking Sara where she was at the approximate time of the murder."

Mary Beth blushed. She considered herself an excellent researcher. Forgetting to ask a suspect where she was at the time of a murder was a blatant omission.

She over-compensated for that omission at noon when she and Tony met with Clara for the picnic they had proposed. The seldom-used gazebo at the far end of the winding path provided the three of them with privacy and comfort. As soon as they were seated around the wrought-iron table, Mary Beth charged in, "Clara, where were you at the time of the murder?"

Tony preferred subtler methods. He had borrowed the bottle of Balvenie from the Prince George House bar and liberally splashed some of it into the coffee carafe he had brought along as his contribution to their al fresco lunch.

Clara side-stepped Mary Beth's abrupt time-of-the-murder question. "Mary Beth, are you trying to trick me? I'm the one who writes mystery novels. I know those traps about the time of the murder. I don't know what time it was committed any more than you do. But I spent all night in the Melville suite with Sara. We worked for a while on a bottle of scotch and on our new book. No, I'm not going to tell you anything about it," she responded to what she wrongly perceived as their intense curiosity about her forthcoming novel.

Tony turned the conversation back to Clara, urging her to finish her coffee and the narrative of her evening's adventures. "Then I read for a while and went to bed. Oh, I talked with Earl, that's my husband, a little earlier. We talk every night." She smiled at her inquisitors, "Love continues even when you've reached the advanced age of 55."

Not wanting to hear details of Clara's love-life, Mary Beth interrupted with a series of questions about the crime. "Do you have any theories about how this murder was committed? Or why? Or when?"

"Hold it, Mary Beth, you, too, Tony. This is a picnic, not a police interrogation. Did Sara or Hans tell you Sara's idea? She's the smart one, you know."

"No, we just talked with Sara, and she told us everyone had a motive, but she didn't go any further than that. On the other hand," Mary Beth again was embarrassed to be reminded about her sleuthing abilities, or lack thereof. "We didn't ask very many questions, did we, Tony?"

Clara didn't give Tony a chance to respond. She had something important to say: "Well, when Sara was talking with Hans and me, she made a big point about how important Marian's well-positioned body and well-made up face were. She thought, for a corpse, Marian was pretty eloquent."

"'Oh eloquent, just, and mighty death,' " Tony quoted. "Sir Walter Raleigh, in case you didn't know."

"Tony, did you ever think of the perennial pain you give people with your quotidian quotations?"

"They're his native language, Clara."

"Look, if you ladies are going to talk about me instead of to me, I don't have to be here. I'm leaving."

"Tony, Clara, let's all calm down." Mary Beth tried to bring order to a conversation that was getting out of hand. "We've all been under terrific stress. First, we're the guests of electronic peeping-toms; then we're conceivably living with a murderer.

"Tony's quote happens to be an appropriate description of Marian's death. 'Eloquent' and 'mighty' to be sure," Mary Beth nodded her agreement. "If we could only figure out who thought it was a just penalty for something real or imagined that Marian did.

"Sara's right. Our best clue is Marian's position. Her well made-up face, the elegant Perla nightgown. Who would go to all of that trouble?"

"It must be a woman," Clara said, calm now and taking a bite of her sandwich. She motioned toward Tony and the scotch, "Would you pour me another cup of that excellent coffee, Tony?

"Who else but a woman could have done all that?" She continued with stronger emotion. "Besides, from my experience, limited to writing, to be sure, I'm positive it was a case of poison. And poison is a woman's weapon. I've done research on every tool any of our characters could use for murder" she said to her astounded audience. "Believe me, I can tell you a little about poisons. According to the FBI, the three deadliest substances in the world are, in descending order of lethality, plutonium, botulism toxin, and ricin. But you know that," she added, sure that they didn't and secretly admiring her own arcane knowledge. Taking a cup of that delicious coffee with her, she left Mary Beth and Tony before she lost her advantage.

Mary Beth shrugged her shoulders, "She certainly knows more about poisons than I do. The question is, has she ever used that knowledge outside of her fictive writing? I'll see what Hans makes of all this."

A little later, when Mary Beth saw Hans in the hallway and reported the Sara and Clara conversations to him, she thanked him for suggesting that they interview the two women separately. "You're right, Hans. They might be a twosome for writing, but they're quite different women in real life. Smarter, too, than all of those cat and mouse books would lead you to believe. We did learn some things from them individually that we might not have learned if we had seen them together. Mainly, that we haven't given enough thought to the positioning of Marian's body. Now we should talk with Buck. It'll probably mean a second lunch, but detective work takes sacrificing. Are you in on this one?"

"Mary Beth, I never developed the art of small talk. And you'll need some friendly chatter before you leap into interrogations. You and Tony get the information. I'll analyze it. Analysis and criticism are my strong points. I'm sure I'll be able to construct a plausible theory when we, again I mean you and Tony and I, get all of the facts together.

"You and I need to spend some time together too, Mary Beth," he said in a low-voiced aside. "Murder isn't the only subject on my mind. I don't think it's the only subject on yours either."

For someone who spent most of her career lecturing, Mary Beth became surprisingly inarticulate—unless you count that blush.

Chapter Twenty-two

Friday, early afternoon

Energized because they were nearing the end of the interview process, Mary Beth and Tony went looking for Buck. It was not a difficult task; from the corridor they could hear him typing away in his studio. Mary Beth turned Buck's name into a question as she knocked, "Buck?"

"Don't stand on any ceremony. Push open the door and come on in," he called out.

"I wasn't sure you'd want me to barge in," Mary Beth said as she pushed at the door.

"Who wouldn't want you to come into his bedroom?" was Buck's rejoinder before he sheepishly realized that she wasn't alone.

Mary Beth and Tony entered Buck's darkly masculine room. *Had each room been decorated with its occupant in mind?* Mary Beth wondered, then thought of her own room across the hall with papers, books, and journals overflowing their stacks on the floor. That lived-in look was the result of her own personal touch. The room hadn't started out that way. A few days ago, it had the impersonal look found in a new bed and breakfast. The room was painted a boring, institutional beige, relieved by a dozen pillows carelessly tossed around to mimic hospitable charm.

"Buck, we were thinking of taking a break for a cappuccino or something stronger and going into town," Mary Beth said. "How about joining us? It'll be good to get out of this atmosphere of continuous crime for a while."

"Hans and I went to the Prince of Wales Pub one afternoon. The atmosphere is faker than my cowboy accent," Buck replied, laughing at himself, "but the food isn't bad. And I haven't had lunch, though I'm not about to try their Special Stonehenge Sandwich," he quickly added as they walked downstairs together.

The three were not surprised to find Gary and his cab outside the front door, nor were they surprised to find in the course of the drive to the restaurant that Gary was also a writer. Eco-socialist thrillers were his specialty. He drove with one hand on the wheel and began to read from a tract he was holding with the other, "The unique water and land forms of Ohio and the rest of the Great Lakes region are a striking legacy of past climates."

"I know that the Ice Age left some beautiful fertile land here in northeastern Ohio, but still, two hands on the steering wheel, please, Gary," Mary Beth corrected him in her best school-marmish voice.

The mumble that was Gary's negative rejoinder sounded almost like Marx's Revolutionary call, "Abolition of the wages system."

He was certainly calling for the abolition of something, which made his three passengers happy to get out of the taxi when they arrived at the Pub. "Let's not take too much time over lunch," Buck admonished. "Why? Cause 'meanwhile, back at the ranch,' as they say, there's work waitin' for me to do. Don't get me wrong. I'm looking forward to a drink away from that ghost town of a house. Do you notice how fast writers are disappearing?

"I aim to be polite and enjoy your company, but since Marian was killed, I've written one-hundred pages that just rock. I want to get back to them while I'm still swingin' in the saddle."

"Marian's death inspired you?" Tony asked as they took seats in a dark wooden booth.

"That's harsh, dude," Buck began.

Before he could complete his answer to the perceived attack, the Ohio serving wench came to tell them of the day's "olde tyme" specials, which they ignored in favor of hamburgers. *That early lunch wasn't very satisfying*, Mary Beth made excuses to herself. *Anyway. this is more companionable.*

While the three of them waited discreetly to be served, Buck carried on a monologue. "Did you hear the one about the small cowboy sitting at the bar nursing a drink? A big old cowpoke came in, grabbed the drink from him and chugged it. The little wrangler said, 'That finishes it. I've had the world's worst day. First my house caught fire, then my bull ran away, then I decided to commit suicide and you upped and drank my bourbon with poison.' " Tony gave him an I've-heard-that-before look. Mary Beth, more polite, rewarded him with a smile.

After the server brought their lager in imitation Toby mugs and left them alone, they continued their discussion.

Buck felt it necessary to explain his small cowboy/big cowboy joke. "I knew you didn't want to talk with that gal around. I've always got a Western joke at the ready for something like this. So, what' up? Is this some kind of a show-down about me?" He leaned forward as he asked.

"It's about Marian, Buck," Tony said. "We want to find out as much as we can about her and thought you could help."

"I know what you all know. Plus I asked Lois a few important questions that you skipped over. So I also know that the coroner's examination showed that Marian hadn't been violated."

"Except, of course, by being killed," Tony interjected.

Mary Beth brought the conversation back to where she wanted it: "The first time I saw you, Buck, you were talking with Marian and neither one of you looked very happy about it. That was at the meet-and-greet cocktail party when we first arrived at Lakeville. Can you believe it? That was just Sunday. You know, I feel like I'm a different person than I was when I came here on Sunday. I'll bet everyone does."

"I remember that conversation, Mary Beth. I'm not that old. And I wasn't unhappy about seeing Marian there; I knew she was coming. But I was angry and I'm still angry every time I think of her."

"Not the way to talk about the dead. My bad, again. That's getting to be my mantra, isn't it?" he apologized.

"Even though I didn't and still don't like Marian and I personally think she deserved to die, I never would have killed her."

"Would you care to explain?" Tony asked.

"If you've talked with anyone else about Marian, and I'm sure you have, then you know she's a user.

Mary Beth and Tony nodded agreement.

"Mare and I were friends, well, more than friends, in my rodeo days. I introduced her to my good old buddy Larry who did a singing clown act. Lariat Larry, he called himself. You have to be a pretty good horseman to make those rodeo fans laugh, and he was, but he was never one of the top rodeo hands in the world.

"Larry wrote his own songs. I thought that Marian with her writer's eye could critique them, make them even better, so I gave her some of his songs to look at. Larry and I trailed together at the beginning, but after a while, we were riding different circuits. The next thing I hear, his horse threw him and trampled him. He died instantly, leaving a wife and two babies. Believe me, rodeo clowns don't have retirement plans and insurance policies. It costs a lot to go on the road if you don't have sponsors and you have to pay your own way, the way Larry did. All he would have had was his writing. But Marian had his writing. She turned those songs into her first children's stories and broke into publishing that way. Trying to get her to commit to any royalties for Larry's family was like trying to nail Jell-o to a tree. She never gave a word of credit; never gave a cent to Katie, his wife, or to the two kidders. They're O.K. When I made it big, I started a fund for them," he said. "No way to prove anything against her. I must be the only one who knows. That's what I was talking to her about on Sunday night, about making restitution. She owes Lariat Larry a public debt of gratitude and she owes his family money, moola, big bucks. Nothing'll ever come of it now."

"I guess you had every reason to want her to be alive," Mary Beth said as she wrapped up half of her hamburger to take back to the house.

Buck hadn't finished his tirade against Marian. "She's a spoiler even today. This whole idea of 'Ohio Creates,' would have been so great if she hadn't upped and gotten herself killed. Roping people into a place away from our usual hang-outs, reducing distraction (no cows or calves), and promoting exchanges across different writing disciplines would have had saleable results. For me, anyway. Now look at us."

Tony looked and saw Mary Beth wrapping up that sandwich. "What are you doing, Mary Babe, Cook is a food-pusher, an over-eating enabler; you're not in Midfield any more! This is one week when you don't have to stretch your salary."

"Oh, I was brought up to 'waste not, want not,' and to turn off the lights when I leave a room. and all of that good stuff that's gone out of style."

"Exercise is in style," Tony segued. "Let's walk back to the House. It'll do us good after those massive hamburgers, and I don't feel like proving my proletarian roots to the cab driver."

"Maybe we didn't give him a big enough tip," Mary Beth said.

"No, he doesn't take tips, something to do with class-devisiveness. At least, he's consistent."

But even contemplating Gary's power to the proletariat couldn't turn the conversation away from Marian. Buck picked up the subject again. "You know, folks, there had to be malice aforethought here. There was no spontaneous violence; it was premeditation if I ever saw it. That's murder one. We're talking about a serious killer."

"Like it could have been an un-serious killer. What are you saying, Buck?"

"I'm sayin' it's high noon in Hadleyville and we ought to have our symbolic six-shooters at the ready."

"I never knew Hadleyville was the name of the town where Sheriff Gary Cooper had his shoot-out. So this lunch-time investigation wasn't a total waste, after all!"

They paused in their walk to look at four Andean Indians, complete with ponchos, sitting on a corner and playing pipes. "Who would expect to see this in Lakeville, Ohio?" Mary Beth asked.

"I've traveled around the world," Buck answered, "and there's not a country that doesn't have a group of these pipe players serenading pedestrians during tourist season. The population of the whole Andean mountain range and half of Peru must be decimated."

They finished their short stroll in silence; downtown only extended a few blocks in either direction from the Pub. When they separated in the entrance hall of Prince George House, Buck said, "I've got work to do. If I rustle up any more information, I'll get it to you. I don't mind facin' down a good-for-nothing villain, but I sure don't like this not knowing."

"We have to join forces," Tony agreed for himself and for Mary Beth. "We have to exchange information with each other.

"Our problem is we don't really have any information to exchange," he added in a secretive aside to Mary Beth. "And I'm not sure anymore about Buck. Don't you think its passing strange that his whole speech about not killing Marian depends on the testimony of two people? And they're both dead. Marian and that Lariat Larry"

Buck was already leaving and didn't notice Mary Beth and Tony whispering to each other. He gave a back-hand wave and a "See ya' later."

Tony agreed. That's definitely what would happen.

Chapter Twenty-three

Friday, continued

"What did you think of Buck?" Mary Beth asked after he had left. "I can't see whether Lariat Larry's being alive or dead has any bearing on this case. Honestly, I wouldn't put it past Buck to have invented that whole Larry story to make himself look good. I will say that Buck's concept of sartorial splendor gives me pause. But it's not a crime. For all of his talk and bravado, I really don't think he could fill the bill for a desperado, do you?"

"Who could?"

"That's our problem. I have Hans's cell number. Let's call him to join us and see what we've got."

"No one's in the library. We can sit there for a while and make a chart of suspects. I'm an engineer and I like charts, just the way you like footnotes!"

Mary Beth and Tony sat side-by-side at one of the well-lit library tables while Mary Beth called upstairs. Hans said he'd be down in a minute. Tony used the time to carefully align all papers and magazines to the right angles of the table. Mary Beth pretended to re-write her notes. Hans arrived with a business-like notebook in hand and subtly staked out his claim to Mary Beth by taking the power chair directly opposite her. As Mary Beth watched him watching her, her inner optimist took over, *This relationship isn't finished. Maybe we could keep in touch after this is all over* . . .

Tony smiled internally. He knew what kind of maneuvering was going on. But in a very un-Tony manner, he restrained himself and did not show any emotion on the surface.

Instead, he took charge. "You talk, Mary Best. Get into your academic lecturing mode. Hans, you take notes. I'll visualize and, if we're lucky, I'll be able to make a few charts."

"Tony, you know darn well I'm not a lecturer. I like to interact with my classes. Students learn much more when they help with discovery. So, if you don't mind I'll interact with you the same way."

"Mary Babe, have I ever objected when you wanted to interact with me?"

"Tony, this is a murder. We aren't playing Nancy Drew and The Hardy Boys. Sorry, Hans."

Hans ignored the by-play and made a suggestion that was immediately adopted, "We have to start some place. Let's start by eliminating suspects."

He plunged ahead, "It seems that Nikki and Malcolm's crime of videotaping all of us without our knowledge is disgusting and illegal, but, according to the police, has nothing to do with the murder and, in fact, provides them with a fool-proof alibi. As we know, they were getting their kicks by videotaping themselves at the same time. So that lets them out."

Mary Beth continued, "Cook and Gary from Indiana, the taxi driver (I guess he's her boyfriend, right?) can be eliminated, too. They're the professional village characters, neo-Marxist criticism and all. The local residents, including Detective Lois and her whole Lois Club, would string us up if we dared to point a finger of suspicion at them.

"Every town has Andean pipers, but who else has Cook and Gary?" she asked.

"They seem to be Lakeville's only tourist attraction," Hans agreed, adding "though being such well-known local personalities would make a good cover if you were going to commit a crime, wouldn't it?

"But what about other household help?" he probed.

"Oh, two townies come in to clean," Mary Beth explained. "They're a mother-daughter team, somehow related to Cook. I think this whole town shares the same DNA."

"That's no proof of innocence," Tony cut in.

"The daughter was hired first, but it turns out that she's allergic to dust, so she brought in her mother to do the initial cleaning. Then she tidies up."

"What? A cleaning woman allergic to dust? Isn't that a career challenge?"

"Yes, but that's not all. The mother has arthritis, so can't clean anything that she has to reach by stretching an arm or bending a knee."

Tony smiled, "This is turning into a dirty shaggy dog story. But it does explain the clean swath going only through the middle of all of the downstairs rooms. It doesn't explain if they're innocent or not."

"Lois swears by them. By their characters, not their cleaning abilities," Mary Beth laughed.

"If we eliminate all four of them," Mary Beth continued, "that brings us to our happy few, our group of writers. I know I didn't do it."

"For Pete's sake, Mary B. I didn't either," Tony blurted out.

"I know, Tony," Mary Beth said.

"And I certainly didn't," said Hans, through teeth clenched at the idea.

Tony calmed him. "There are some things I don't like about you, Hans." He looked at Mary Beth. "But I'm sure you didn't murder Marian. You might want to get back at her, but I've been Googling you; you're too subtle for murder. You get back at people with your pen."

Mary Beth had been leaning over the table. She sat up straight. The need to know why Marian was murdered washed over her at unexpected times. This was one of them. She tried to explain to Tony and Hans, "Each time I walk into my room and see Marian's pashmina shawl, still draped over the back of my chair, I get this strong emotion of sympathy with Marian. I expect it then. But I get it other times, too, like now. It reminds me that I have to know what happened." Mary Beth was never really surprised by the emotion. She knew she had to learn why? And by whom?

Though she knew she was pointing out the obvious, May Beth pushed the conversation in the direction it had to go, "That leaves Clara, Sara, and Buck."

"A trio of unlikely murderers if I ever saw one," Hans amended.

"Have you ever seen one?" Tony asked.

Hans shook his head.

"Then we have to go with what we've got. Go on, Mary Best."

"O.K. I've tried to tease apart all of their ramblings to tell you what I really hear. First, we have Sara. And we have to accept that Sara was absolutely right, even if she is Sara. She pointed out what we should be treating as the biggest clue, Marian's immaculate make-up and positioning. Why would she be helping us if she's the murderer?"

"Maybe that's why, so she'll look innocent," Hans explained. "She is a writer, after all, someone who arranges settings and eccentricities."

"I can't believe she's that devious."

"What about Clara?" Hans asked. "She's Sara's alibi and Sara's hers. What do we know about her? She likes her liquor, knows some peculiar facts—like her riff on Lois Clubs—so maybe she knows about poisons. But her physical un-fitness is so apparent. She gets out of breath just going up and down the front stairs. I don't see how she'd have the energy to murder any one."

"How much energy do you need to poison anyone?" was Tony's interjection.

"You're right again. I suppose not much." Hans said, concluding his Sara-monologue. "Still, Clara writes mysteries and we all know that the writers of mysteries play games with their readers. Maybe that's what she's doing with us."

"Writers play fair," Mary Beth argued. "They give the readers clues. All she gave us was Buck." Mary Beth corrected herself. "No, I think that was Sara. But what about Buck?"

"You mean it's the shoot out at the O.K. Corral?" Tony interjected. It'll be show-down, if not hoe-down, time for our favorite buckaroo."

"Tony. Do I have to keep telling you? Murder is serious business."

"So is humor, Mary Beth," Hans carefully chided her.

For the first time, Tony looked at Hans with a little respect. But he kept the conversation on target. "What do you think of Buck as a villain?"

"Hard to picture it, isn't it," Mary Beth commented, "except that we don't really know anything about him before he changed his name, back when he was plain Harrison Carter in his pre-Buck days."

"My turn to do some work on this committee," Hans said. "I'll do the research on Buck and a few others. I'm good at doing computer checks beyond Google, plus I'll go to the Lakeville Library and access their search engines. This is a wealthy community with a library that's bound to be hooked up to the On-line Computer Library Center, one of the few services the Prince George House doesn't offer."

Correctly assuming agreement, Hans gathered up his papers, pushed back his chair, and left.

Tony held Mary Beth back. "While you and Hans were talking, I made a chart, just the way I told you I would. It's simple, but I think it will be a help. First, I listed all of the people I think we can safely eliminate.

Suspect	Alibi	Conclusion
Malcolm Nikki	Police say tapes show they were otherwise occupied	Alibis verified by video & Arrested on voyeurism, porn & other charges
Mary Beth	Asleep. I know she's O.K.	Fahgedaboudit
Tony	Not in Lakeville. I know I'm O.K.	Fahgedaboudit.
Hans	Buck in library is his alibi Weak motive. He's O.K., too	Fahgedaboudit
Cook Gary & cabbie	Were with group of Marxist Critics at supposed time of murder	Alibis hold
H. Buck	Hans in library is his alibi	Pending investigation
Sara	Clara is her alibi. Emphasized eloquent and elegant corpse position	Doesn't seem possible
Clara	Sara is her alibi. Not strong enough for murder. Poison doesn't take strength.	Worth more investigation

Mary Beth quickly scanned Tony's chart. "This is great, Tony. I think it will really help us. Could you go to the office and make copies for Hans and me? I'll study mine later and we can talk about it seriously."

Chapter Twenty-four

Friday afternoon

"Mary Babe, I'll copy the chart later, but remember I told you I had something to show you? I could start by giving you a five-minute crash-course in engineering so you'd understand my discovery." Tony didn't wait for Mary Beth's agreement to begin his lecture. "I'm sure I've told you my math teacher always insisted geometry would come in handy. I even 'learned by geometric scale/to take the size of pints of ale.' Me and Samuel Adams."

"Yes, Tony, you've told me about it a number of times."

Tony shifted gears. Mary Beth was obviously uninterested in Engineering 101, no matter how well-prepared he was as a teacher. O.K., his presentation was adaptable. "At your service, ma'am. Long story short, and will be accompanied by our own physical diagrams. For the first one, let's stand in the center of the reception hall."

They walked over together and stood facing the entrance door. Tony made a sweeping gesture, "What do you see?"

"I see a good-sized corridor or passageway leading from the front door to where we're standing in the entrance hall. From experience in using both rooms, I know a coat closet is on one side of the corridor and a powder room is on the other.

"Do you want me to go on?" In answer to Tony's nod, she did. "On one side of the space where the passageway becomes the entrance hall that we're standing in right now, I see a bust of Mr. Syberstone sporting a cowboy hat, which I'm sure he never wore. Buck's way of announcing he's in the house!"

"Yes. Yes. Go on."

"On the other side of that space where the passageway becomes the entrance hall, there's a framed mirror that . . . Oh, I forgot to put on lipstick. Just a moment, Tony, I want to freshen up a bit."

"Mary Beth, you look great, for Pete's sake. I'm trying to show you something. Did you notice that the bust is placed in a niche in the wall that's about two feet deep? Now look at the mirror that's supposed to balance it on the same wall, but on the other side of the passageway; it's set so that it is flush with the wall. One side has a deep indentation, the opposite side just a few inches."

"Naturally, when you point it out, I can see it, Tony. But honestly, Hon, I've seen things a tad odder than that in my life. Anyway, asymmetrical is in."

"For all I know, it was in when Syberstone's house was built, too. Queen Anne architecture is supposed to be full of surprises, but not like this."

Mary Beth couldn't resist cutting in, "Do you mean surprises like the house's historically accurate Queen Anne-style, detached three-car garage?"

For once, Tony didn't smile at Mary Beth's joke. He was unusually stern. "Mary Beth, when I started to study the house, I could see immediately that volumetrically some of this space couldn't be accounted for.

"Come on. For our second physical diagram, let's stand at the front door and look into the house." In his excitement, he pushed Mary Beth along until they reached the front door and turned to face the corridor leading to the entrance hall. He repeated his sweeping gesture. "Now what do you see? What does each indentation back up against? Look, directly behind the bust of Syberstone, our patriarch, is the coat closet. Go ahead, walk in. Walk in. Yes, it goes all the way back to the three-foot indentation needed to frame the bust.

"Now, let's look at the other side, behind the mirror."

"I feel like Alice in Wonderland," Mary Beth was almost gleeful as she walked out of the coat closet and started toward the powder room.

"Mary Beth, it's my time to say, this is something serious."

"Sorry, Tony." Mary Beth re-arranged her face into its studious mode. With her hand on the doorknob, she said, more to herself than to Tony, "I'm entering the powder room that's directly behind the mirror. I'll see if anyone's using it before you come in, Tony."

"I don't care," Tony said as he followed her into the small guest bathroom. I want to show you that if you go all the way to the rear, it has a three-foot indentation, too, just like the coat closet does. We've seen that's the indented three feet for Syberstone's bust. You have to ask, what's the indented three feet for in the powder room? The mirror on the other side of it only needs a few inches." As they paced it off, Mary Beth realized that Tony's calculations were absolutely right. The wall at the end of the powder room left three feet not accounted for.

Tony wanted to be sure Mary Beth understood. "You know I always plot everything out on graph paper," he said. Look at this, Mary Best." He took a folded piece of graph paper out of his pocket and showed her the simple diagram he had drawn.

"Wow. It's so obvious when you map it out like that. The coat closet and the powder room have the exact same dimensions, but at the end of the powder room are three unused blocks on your graph paper, the three feet we can't account for. Or can we? Tony, do you think there's a secret closet there or a tunnel or . . ."

"Yes. Mary Babe. A staircase." Tony's adrenaline rush had him literally jumping around the small space. "This engineering problem's a blast."

"I'll take your word for it, but if a staircase ever was really hidden there, it's pretty well sealed over with coats of plaster now."

"That's what it looks like, doesn't it? Prince George House really rocks, Mary Beth. It's full of surprises. Surprises that your close friend, this engineering genius, is having one helluva good time uncovering.

"I did the easiest kind of empirical research possible. I pressed my weight against various wood panels looking for one that would give. Before I found one with wiggle-room, I had to try the main room, dining room, and especially the library because that's where staircases are always hidden in books and movies. Then I came to the entrance hall. I could feel that some of these wall sections were hinged."

Tony's height and strength came in handy. As he spoke, he lifted the large oval mirror and carefully leaned it against a wall. The back of the mirror and the wall were covered with only slightly disturbed dust. Tony had been very careful to leave his discovery as he had found it.

Mary Beth coughed and said, "At least, the cleaning ladies are consistent. Their motto must be 'Never dust under what you can dust around.' "

Tony didn't respond. He touched a button. Flush with the wall, it was almost invisible. Under recently-disturbed, obscuring dust, the button needed only a slight painted disguise to match the marbleized walls. With his touch, a portion of the chair rail popped out. It served as the handle that allowed him to disclose the hidden door. When he pulled, the door swung back to reveal a small opening, adequate for a normal person. Tony re-hung the mirror and stooped to enter the enclosure. Mary Beth, who was short enough to stand upright, followed immediately behind him. He reached around her to close the door. No tell-tale signs were left in the entrance hall.

"Can you see, Mary Babe? These are rather old Soss invisible hinges. They might be the original design Soss patented in 1903. That means a little home improvement was done a while after the house was built. But the staircase is original to the house; it's beautifully built—made so that you can ascend quite rapidly and quietly within such a confined space. The stairs are only about eighteen inches wide. No problem if you walk sideways."

But it was dark, so Mary Beth and Tony ascended slowly, feeling their way through the occasional cobweb and up the stairs. "I'll bring a flashlight if we do this again," Tony whispered.

They reached the top, and Tony, still in the lead, opened the door. Mary Beth followed, squinting against the light coming in from behind the large flowered chintz curtain. The Longfellow Room.

Chapter Twenty-five

Friday afternoon, continued

They were in Marian's room. Though it was sealed and crime-taped on the exterior door and walls, there, inside the eerily empty room, stood Mary Beth and Tony staring wide-eyed at each other.

Mary Beth looked around her with amazement.

Tony beamed with pride of discovery.

"This is how he did it, Tony."

"I think that this is how *she* did it, Mary Best. I always think of poison as a woman's weapon and I think I've figured out which woman, not that she looks like she knows anything about cosmetics. But what guy could put on make-up the way Marian or Marian's corpse was wearing it? Is there such a word as necrocosmetology? Unless he was an undertaker," he answered his own question.

"Does anyone have a background in . . ."

Mary Beth did a double-take, interrupting herself. "What did you mean, you know who did it?"

Tony pulled a plastic bag out of his back jean pocket and handed it to her.

"It's a dirty button, Tony."

"A dirty button? Mary Babe, this is an outward and visible sign of someone's inward and until-now invisible sneakiness! I found it on the staircase."

"Tony, it could have been lying there in the dirt for ten years."

"Look again."

Mary Beth re-examined the button. "It's decorated with a hand-painted—I don't believe it, a hand-painted cat."

"Anyway, Babe, this secret staircase is important, but it isn't how he or she did it. If it was a well enough disguised poison, no one had to sneak in to administer it."

"But Tony this is most certainly how Sarah or someone got into Marian's room after the poison took effect. Someone knew how long to wait before coming back to the room to clean her up. But we don't belong here. I'm getting nervous. Let's get out."

They quietly left the room through the newly discovered doorway, cleverly hidden under the Longfellow Room's heavily flowered wallpaper, and descended the secret staircase. They waited for a moment at the bottom to make sure no sounds were coming from the entrance hall. The staircase was Tony's discovery. He and Mary Beth wanted to choose the right people to hear about it and the right time to tell about it. This wasn't it. When they were sure no one was in the entrance hall, they re-entered the room, closing the hinged section of the panel behind them.

"Tony, you're an architectural genius," Mary Beth said as she brushed a little dust off of his shoulder.

"Not quite," he answered with what she thought was becoming modesty, until he added, "But as I've mentioned, I am an engineering genius."

"Whatever this staircase means, Tony, we have to tell Lois ASAP. Maybe one of us should stay here to keep watch."

"For what? Mary Babe, I'm willing to bet that whoever was smart enough to find and use the staircase was smart enough not to leave fingerprints or other clues behind, and, for sure, whoever it was, he, she, or it is smart enough to stay away from that mirror now."

Mary Beth and Tony walked toward the front door as sedately as they could manage under the circumstances. Tony automatically headed towards his bicycle parked next to Mary Beth's PT Cruiser under the *porte cochère*. One look from Mary Beth and he changed direction, sliding into the passenger side of her car as she opened the door on the driver's side.

They found Lois in her office, ready to trade information. As a consummate professional, she never would have phrased it that way. But the information Lois's office had just received from the Poison Center was going to be public in a few hours. When Tony told her his staircase news and gave her the bagged button, she took a slight risk. She used her Poison Center information to thank Mary Beth and Tony for their amazing discoveries. The button was definitely a clue. But to what? And uncovering the hidden staircase was great. The rumor of one had been circulating ever since Prince George was built. It had been embellished and used to illustrate other rumors, but no one had discovered it before. Lois corrected herself. *Yes. Someone else at Prince George House had discovered it before Tony had.*

Lois turned to the task at hand. "We have learned," she said, "that Marian Rogers was killed by a powerful drug. A non-volatile, organic poison was used, one that we have yet to identify. We do know that it was probably a powder that could be absorbed by the skin or ingested easily. For example, if some of the powder were on your hand and you wiped your mouth . . "

"Finger licking," Mary Beth cried out. "Remember how Marian turned the pages of *Little Boy Blue* when she was first looking at it?"

Lois and Tony's faces reflected the same big question mark.

"I forgot. Neither of you were there. The first day at Prince George House, I got a package, a book to review. It was kiddie lit, so I passed it on to Marian. I noticed how she licked a finger as she turned the pages. She'd lick her finger, turn a page, lick her finger again, turn another page. Yuck, I hate that habit. But she must have started to poison herself immediately. No wonder she didn't feel good at dinner that first night."

"Are you saying . . ."

"Yes, the substance, the poison, whatever it is, had to have been transferred from those not so innocent pages of *Little Boy Blue*. It had to have been on the upper right-hand corner of some or maybe all of the pages."

"If you're right, what does that mean, Mary Best? That someone was trying to kill you? You said that the book was addressed to you. Are you saying that Marian is the unintended victim?"

"No, that's impossible. Anyone who knows me well enough to want to kill me would know that kiddie lit isn't my field. I'm known for literally not touching the stuff, calling it pandering to children. Sending the book to me must have been a delay tactic, some kind of a distraction, just so we'd be confused the way we are now.

"And Marian had a house-full of enemies. Every writer here wanted to kill her. But no one wanted to *kill* her."

"Mary Babe this means that the murderer might not be one of your writing pals up at the House. Maybe Marian's murder was by an outsider, the outsider who mailed you the package. Let's get everyone together and tell them."

Lois had allowed her two co-detectives and still-suspects to talk in front of her as much as they wanted, hoping to pick up more information. She started to stop their spreading any news and/or theories, but realized quickly that shaking up the inhabitants of Prince G. House with news about the staircase and poison might be the impetus she needed to solve this case.

So, Lois held her tongue, saying only "Goodbye" as Mary Beth and Tony departed.

As soon as they left, Lois, who was beginning to think of herself as garbage scrounger in-chief, went back to her workroom next to her office. More like a C.S.I. than a detective, she had collected each fragment of light blue printed material from the destroyed book. This was no easy task as the scraps had been distributed among trash containers in the kitchen, library, and some bedrooms. Someone had very deliberately "hidden" the fragments of the few missing pages in this way. Lois carefully plucked each piece of paper from the garbage with a tweezers-like instrument. Just as carefully she pieced the complicated jig-sawed-looking bits of paper together and glued them on substantial backings before sending them to the poison lab. The whole process was compounded by the plastic gloves Lois wore at all times during her garbage search. She, of course, did not want to disturb any finger prints or other evidence. In addition, she didn't have to take any courses in garbology to know that if her theory (maybe Mary Beth and Tony had helped a little), if her theory was true, if, in fact, some of the pages had been impregnated with poison, she was following the right path (*again*).

audrey lavin

Chapter Twenty-six

Friday night, later

Seen through the mullioned library windows, the darkening sky made a melodramatic background for Mary Beth and Tony's hurried convocation of Prince George House's resident writers.

"We have something very important to tell you," Mary Beth started. Tony interrupted, "No, *show* you. Follow me."

"A little melodramatic, isn't he?" Buck muttered to Hans.

"What do you think this whole week has been? Theater in the raw."

When the five writers, followed by a curious Cook, reached the entrance hall mirror, Tony stopped them. They stood waiting in a rough semi-circle with Tony in the center.

Mary Beth stepped back as Tony lifted the mirror. *It's his show, his discovery,* she thought. *While he demonstrates, I'll just be the interested observer.* Tony placed the mirror on the floor and paused for effect. He made a dramatically vigorous arm gesture in the direction of the variegated marble wall where the mirror had hung, then let his arm drop slowly to the chair-rail. When he finally pressed the buttons and the section of wall swung out, his action was greeted by gasps and screams, plus laughter of astonished appreciation, and a "Well, I'll be hog-tied" from Buck.

Tony beckoned. Clara, Sara, Hans, and Buck followed him into the small stairwell entrance with Mary Beth bringing up the rear. It was a tighter fit for some than it was for others, but for Tony's apprehensive followers, it was a quick trip up the stairs. As far as Mary Beth could see from scrutinizing reactions, not one of the writers had expected the destination to be the Longfellow Room. In fact, after the shock of a murder and of finding a hidden staircase, the flowered decorating scheme of that room seemed almost an affront to all.

"What in the hell does this mean?" Hans voiced the question on everyone's mind.

"One thing it means is that an outsider could have come into the house and gone upstairs without any one of us hearing a thing," said Sara, realizing almost as she made her statement that the secret staircase also invalidated the alibis of the five writers there, including her own.

"Someone or, for all we know, two-someones," Buck said looking at Clara and Sara, "someone didn't have to use the main, squeaky staircase to get to the Longfellow Room. Someone before Tony found that nice and quiet secret in the entrance hall, the secret that leads directly to the room above it.

"I've underestimated you, Tony. Congratulations. Job well done," he added, slapping Tony on the back.

"I can't get my mind around this," Clara said. "It's getting late. Can we think about it tonight and talk about it some more tomorrow? What do some of the implications mean, like our all swearing we didn't hear the stairs creaking Sunday night when Marian was murdered?"

"I'm getting psyched by all of this," Sara said. "That was the name of the poem," she exclaimed. "Remember? 'As I was going up the stair/I met a man who wasn't there./He wasn't there again today./I wish, I wish he'd stay away.' It's getting too true."

"Clara's right," Hans said, trying to calm everyone. "We'll talk about all of this tomorrow after dinner and a good night's sleep."

They silently filed down the center staircase to the entrance hall with the occasional squeak of the treads reminding them of the importance of Tony's discovery. They went into the dining room where Cook had laid out a late, light supper of fruit and sandwiches. Cook had always been independent. Now without Nikki and Malcolm being there to supervise her, she spent more of her time watching the writers than cooking for them.

Some of the writers were dazed. Some were trying to understand what the hidden staircase could mean. Suspicions were rampant; nerves were on edge. With too much to think about, but not much to say to each other, supper was over in a hurry.

Only Buck made an effort to re-establish their community. As she left the dining room, Mary Beth heard him say to Sara, "Did I ever tell you about the time I was sitting in a bar next to this really small cowboy? He had a drink in front of him, and this great big hoss wrangler comes in and . . .

Tony took his sandwich and followed Mary Beth upstairs. After a slight hesitation, he continued to follow her into her room. He looked around. Not unexpectedly, the arm chair and desk chair were full of books and print-outs.

"Did you have a dys-feng shui expert help you make this mess?" Tony asked as he concentrated on straightening her desk. He picked up Mary Beth's tee-shirt and Turkish beads that had been draped over the printer, "Where do these go?"

"Thanks, hon. Put the shirt in the laundry bag." Mary Beth was so tired that her natural smile of appreciation didn't even reach her eyes.

Not noticing, Tony continued to align the computer, pens, and papers on Mary Beth's desk, still looking for, but not finding, what he considered a proper bead-place.

Then he noticed an unexpected and off-putting detail. Looking at the pen and legal pad placed on what he had hoped would be "his" side of the bed, he hesitated, then blurted out, "Mary Babe, were you planning to take notes while. . .?"

"Oh, of course, Tony, I'm a writer and want to capture each experience, even the most personal one, just as it is unfolding."

Tony was taken aback by Mary Beth's derisive tone. He didn't want their relationship to revert to where it had been a week ago.

He beat a retreat, literally by moving toward the door, and emotionally by saying as he left, "C'mon, Hon, the atmosphere in this house is making us all odd and odder. But it can't turn my Mary Best into a grouch."

Mary Beth smiled while she turned off the light. She planned to sit at the window and figure out what the day's events meant. More immediately, she realized, she wanted to tell Tony she was sorry for being so snappy. She was simply over-tired. He would still be in the hall, so she didn't bother turning on the light, just ran over to the door, opened it and stepped into the hallway to call Tony. At least, that was the plan. Instead, a large crash brought Clara, Sara, and Tony on the run.

Mary Beth was sprawled on the floor outside of her door.

A number of exclamations ran together: "What a lot of noise for such a little woman." "Is she hurt?" "That's what she gets for leaving her books all over the place."

"Mary Beth, are you O.K.?" Sara asked.

"I think I hurt my ankle."

"Did you break it? Now we absolutely will have to call Eric."

Clara gave Sara the most significant "shut up" look she could.

Sara whispered back, "Stop it, Clara. Age is just a number."

Clara gave her another look, "And yours should be unlisted."

"No, I think it's just twisted. It'll probably be black and blue later," Mary Beth answered Sara's question, trying to make light of the accident. "I bruise so easily. If you checked finger-prints, you could always tell who pinched me at a party!"

Hearing the commotion, Hans and Buck who had just started a conversation in the library, ran upstairs. Hans took one look at Mary Beth, "Tony you lift Mary Beth by her shoulders, and I'll try to get her legs without hurting her. Let's get her into her bed."

Buck surveyed the situation, "She weren't thrown by no hoss. She obviously tripped over that stack of books outside her door. Should we call a doctor?"

"No, no. I'm all right. Please. I appreciate everything, but if you all will let me be, I think I'll be a lot better by morning."

With murmurings of "Yes, everything's better in the morning," "Hope you're O.K.," and other appropriate sick-room remarks, the writers backed out, almost as if they were taking leave of royalty. Clara, the last person out, left the door slightly open so they could return without making Mary Beth get out of bed.

Some time later, Mary Beth pulled herself out of a semi-sleep. She muttered a blurry voiced "Come in," to what she thought was a knock on the door.

She had heard correctly. It was Hans, "Mary Beth, Cook had some chicken soup in the freezer. I think I got it warm enough in the microwave. I'm not sure it's a cure-all for sprains and bruises, but maybe. More important, I thought I'd stop by to chat. We don't want you to sleep too much in case you have a concussion." Hans did stay a few minutes, keeping the conversation light, away from their personal relationship and away from murders, not an easy task.

A few minutes after he left and just as Mary Beth was beginning to doze off again, she vaguely hear another knock. No longer having the energy to even say "Come in," she gave a grunt of what she hoped sounded like acquiescence.

Tony walked in as quietly as he could and sat on a corner of the bed. "Mary Babe, are you awake enough to understand me? Are you drugged or dopey at all?"

"No, hon, I'm not any dopier than usual. I only took two Tylenol. I'm sleepy, but I understand plenty. Mainly, that I'm paying for my messiness."

"No, Mary Best, that's what I want to talk with you about. I left the room a few minutes before you fell. No books were piled in front of your door then. I sure would have seen them if they'd been there. I couldn't have helped but notice. You know I would have picked them up for you."

Mary Beth sat straight up in bed. "Are you saying that someone put them there? That someone wanted to physically and emotionally trip me up?"

"That's exactly what I'm saying. Have you heard the expression 'opportunistic crime'? That's what this was. Someone saw a sudden chance to warn you or, more likely, to keep you otherwise occupied so you wouldn't spend time looking for Marian's murderer."

"You're clearing my head in a hurry, Tony-Babe, if I can return the compliment. If someone was really out to get me, that means two things: first, we must be getting close. I'll bet that discovery of the staircase frightened someone. Second, maybe Marian's murder is what you called an 'opportunistic crime' too. Maybe someone who didn't like her stumbled on some way to get rid of her and did it."

Mary Beth was too excited to sit still. She tried to get out of bed as she was talking and quickly was reminded why she was there in the first place. "Ouch. I can't put any weight on that ankle, Tony."

He helped her back into bed, "Wait here, Mary Beth. I want you to stay off of your feet. While you're resting, I'll prowl around to see what I can find. Let's not get into a discussion of mundane matters like murder right now. But I have to say one thing. I want you to be aware that tripping you means more than we're getting close to someone who may be an opportunistic killer. It also means that absolutely the killer is in this house; the murderer has to be one of us. Please be careful while I'm gone."

"Tony, have you noticed that you have the worst ways of saying 'goodnight?' Seriously, close my door on the way out. I'm not expecting anyone and I'll sleep better knowing the door is locked."

"Sleep well. One thing you don't have to worry about is the beads that were on your desk. I took them by mistake when I cleaned up but I just put them back. They gave me a rash where I had them wrapped around my wrist. Look at it."

Mary Beth half looked at the reddened wrist and tried to make sympathetic sounds, but couldn't quite pull it off. She was asleep by the time Tony silently closed the door.

Chapter Twenty-seven

Saturday morning

Mary Beth dreamt about Turkey again that night. Saturday morning when she was jolted awake by the cacophony of birdsong, she wondered why she was obsessing about Izmir. Was a nightmare next with those nice Izmirians turning into Iz-murderers?

While she stood on one foot to brush her teeth, she revived bits and pieces of her dreams. Maybe her red toothbrush handle triggered the memory. Whatever the direct cause, the dream fragments coalesced. She remembered now the elusive something that had seemed so important before. It was an image of the dense red clusters of flowers at the stall where she had bought the beads. *Isn't it odd*, she thought, *at the same time you're an actor in your dream, you can be an outside observer and think, "This is important. I should remember it." Now that I finally do remember it, why? What could be so important about those tall clusters of red flowers?*

Still puzzling over her dream, Mary Beth hobbled downstairs. No one else was in the dining room. *Good.* She didn't want to listen to their solicitous remarks, wondering which ones were sincere and which one definitely wasn't. In the hope of continuing her isolation, she took her strongly brewed Scottish Breakfast tea into the garden. Her eyes took a moment to adjust to the brightness of the sun's glistening on the morning dew. It was a joy to be there even though the saturated grass left her gym shoes more than a little damp.

Mary Beth needed to think. She had chosen a corner affording some privacy. No one from the house could see her. But Hans had entered the dining room just as she left and followed her. Looking over her cup of tea, Mary Beth watched him approach. His long, sure strides brought him in front of her before she had time to plan what to say. Leaving her cup and saucer on her chair, she stood up. She was physically conscious of being only inches away from him. He bent down and kissed her, slowly at first, then with a full-body press. Mary Beth was as involved as Hans was. Her body sang.

She pulled away, but not soon enough to even pretend to be saying 'No.' What she said was, "It's only 7 o'clock in the morning," a remark she realized was ridiculous before she finished saying it.

"That was your wake-up call, Mary Beth. I've waited a week for that and I can wait longer to finish it. Think about it," he added with a look that clearly requested some kind of agreement. Mary Beth started to smile, but didn't have time to form her face into either a 'yes' or 'no' look.

Clara and Sara were bristling toward them, unsuccessfully hiding their curiosity. Hans only slightly distanced himself from Mary Beth, sharing her personal space. He was almost confrontational in greeting The Girls.

Sara waved her coffee cup and Clara her half-eaten roll. Hans thought that under the circumstances, their sing-song "Good morning. How are you?" was the epitome of an insincere conventional greeting. But Mary Beth followed their lead and struggled to make light conversation, a social obligation Hans did not share. Mary Beth chose not to tell Clara and Sara or anyone of her suspicions about her fall. Of course, at least one other person didn't need her to tell him (or her?) that it had not been completely accidental. But Mary Beth couldn't determine who that one other person was.

Returning to the house, Mary Beth tried to figure it out, but couldn't. During all of Saturday morning, everyone was properly considerate. She couldn't expect more than that. After Nikki and Malcolm's arrest for invading their guests' privacy and Marian's still unsolved murder, she could hardly expect people to be overwhelmed with her pain from a twisted ankle. No one else connected her tripping over books to the possibility of her tripping over information about the murderer.

On the other side of breakfast, Hans again caught up with Mary Beth limping along a garden path. Mary Beth steeled herself. But no, he just wanted to ask her to go to Cleveland on Sunday afternoon. "When this workshop is over, I'm going to see my brother and his kidders, as I understand you Ohioans say. Come along for the ride. It'll be fun. I promise I'll return you to your little blue Cruiser as intact as you want to be."

Mary Beth's warm smile and reply "Thanks, Hans, I'd like to some other time" disguised her immediate response, *What? Meet the family? What is he thinking*?

Meanwhile, Lois, who knew how to pull strings and bypass red tape, received her Poison Center report early Saturday morning. She had been collecting favors-owed for just such an occasion. She was right (*again*, she thought). On Monday when Marian's body had been sent from Prince George House to the morgue, Lois had ordered samples taken of all body fluids as well as specimens from all of the cadaver's organs and tissues. Lois was determined to have enough materials to make the tests count. And count they did.

The report carried three items of information: It started with the expected comment that the official, complete results of all lab tests would follow. The report continued by verifying that some of the pages of the blue children's book had been carriers of a rare biological poison. *Right—again*, Lois silently congratulated herself. *The murderer is someone who knew that Marian was a finger-lickin' page turner. But who*? The answer to her follow-up question, *What's the poison?* was the third and final item in the report. That rare, previously unknown poison, was identified as ricin.

"Crunch time. This is it," Lois exulted. She turned to her computer, typed in "questions about ricin," and went directly to the website *atsdric@ cdc.gov*

She learned that "500 micrograms of ricin would be enough to kill an adult." And she never saw the necessity to admit to anyone that she had to look up "microgram." *Wow! 500 micrograms is the size of a pin-*

head. Anyone could have smuggled that in. Or, is it possible that someone found a ricin source on the premises? I'll print out this photo of the plant it comes from and see if anyone has seen it growing in the garden.

By the time Lois returned to the house with the evidentiary photograph, everyone was downstairs. Her arrival was as dramatic as usual. Each time she came to the house, the writers expected her to bring the answer to the horrendous crime of Marian's death. Even those teaming up to search for a solution respected Lois's position and looked to her as their leader. Not one of them was experienced in solving real life murders. They were all careful not to look as if they had any experience in committing them either. This morning, Lois's entrance was deliberate. She kept her expression so well controlled that Sara whispered to Clara, "Look at that frizz. Her hair looks more excited than she does. She couldn't be coming here to make an arrest or anything important."

Sandy Archer, Lois's assistant with the eponymous sandy hair and ruddy face waited at the door while she entered slowly, studying the situation and individual faces, all of which seemed to be professing innocence. No clues there. But she had information that would jar if not rip off those professional masks. She asked the writers to convene in the library.

Buck couldn't resist. "Looks like the final round-up," he wise-cracked. Otherwise he was completely unconcerned with the proceedings. Instead, he was caught up in the almost physical pleasure of studying Lois's body language. *Bad cop mode, um um*, he said to himself finding a seat that was next to her.

"I need your help," Lois said. Faces beamed with pride and acquiescence. She took a photograph out of her portfolio and held it up. "Does anyone recognize this plant? And most important, does it grow in the garden here?"

"That's the long stemmed red flowers from my dream," Mary Beth gasped. "I knew they were the aesthetic correlation for something important."

Ms. Know-it-all Professor is going to drag us off to a symbolic wonderland is what Detective Lois thought. What she politely said was, "I am not interested in allegory here. I am interested in this flower. If you know something about it, would you like to explain, Mary Beth?"

"Twice recently I've dreamt that I was back in Izmir, Turkey, at the souk where I bought my beads and those big red flowers, as tall as I am—and I'm almost five foot four . . . "

Lois reached out a calming hand, "Take a deep breath, Mary Beth. We can all see how tall you are. Try to stay with the pertinent facts. We've had enough misdirection in this case."

"Well, that's it. I kept dreaming about those tall red flowers in your picture. I don't know why they would be important—except the man who made the jewelry told me that most of the beads were seeds from that plant."

"Do you still have those beads?" Lois asked.

She had quickly put two and two together and asked for what she intuited would prove to be important evidence. Lois added another step to her arithmetic equation with the thought that the ostensibly sweet and helpful Mary Beth might have a darker side. First, by having a direct connection with the poisoned book and now, the beads. *She's not leaving this room by herself,* Lois decided.

audrey lavin

Chapter Twenty-eight

Saturday, continued

Lois was gradually shedding her good cop persona. "Let's get a move on, Professor Goldberg," she said, taking Mary Beth by the arm. "I'm going with you to your room to fetch the necklace. I want to see it right now. The beads could be seeds from the ricin plant."

Clara turned to Sara with a self-important look that said, "Who's being kicked out of the catbird seat now?"

Sara nodded agreement.

"Look, these can't be the only beads on your string," Tony interrupted the not-so-secret signaling going on in the room. *Mary Beth as a suspect? That would be the ultimate F-word, 'Fiction'.* "There must be other sources of ricin."

Mary Beth, who with Lois was headed toward the stairwell and her room to find the beads, turned back when she heard Tony. She knew that literally he was right. The beads on the broken string weren't the only ones. The necklace wasn't as long as it used to be. Probably some of the beads hadn't been retrieved when they fell in the driveway.

"Let's go, Mary Beth," Lois verbally prodded her.

Mary Beth's response was to walk even more slowly as she led the way to her room. She needed time to think. All of her concentration was taken up with trying to avoid creaky floorboards while favoring her good foot. Still, she managed to tell Lois the story of her tackle and the broken beads in the driveway. She hesitated, not wanting to implicate Hans. *But he's not being accused of anything. He didn't do anything but help me*, she realized and poured out the whole story—almost the whole story. She began with the Jay's streak of blue aggression, but stopped before she got to the immediate attraction she had felt for Hans. *After all, that has no bearing on the case.*

As they entered her room, Mary Beth picked up Marian's cashmere shawl that was still hanging over a chair. She wrapped herself in it, whispering, "This is it, almost." Mary Beth was too pragmatic to believe in spirits, but she felt that the shawl connected her to Marian, that somehow Marian would know. Across the room, she could see the beads where Tony had put them, tied around the reproduction railway desk lamp.

Lois put on latex gloves she had in her pocket and picked up the necklace, "Lovely necklace. I would have bought it myself. But didn't you ever get a rash from wearing it?"

"No," but she remembered who did.

"According to my sources, some people are highly allergic to the castor bean. That's what your beads are, Mary Beth, and that's where ricin comes from."

Mary Beth wasn't listening; she was thinking of the slight rash Tony developed from handling the necklace in her room and the similar heavy one Hans had shown her on the picnic. *It couldn't be Tony. It couldn't be Hans.*

Lois planned to follow all clues. No slip-shod detective work for her, but first things first. She wanted to discuss her findings with Sandy, who was downstairs keeping his eye on the rest of the suspects. She also wanted to keep Mary Beth at her side, discreetly under observation, so she took Mary Beth back down to the library and deposited her on the easily visible couch. Lois then took Sandy aside to inform him of the castor beans and Tony's and Hans's telling rashes. Knowing that Tony supposedly hadn't even been in Lakeville when Marian was murdered, she gave immediate orders to her uniformed assistant to search Hans's room first.

But she had so many unanswered questions. She was afraid of moving too quickly. She had already been disappointed in thinking that the yellow rubber gloves were a clue. Who would have guessed that a Marxist cook would want to protect her dainty hands from dish water?

So Lois started to make a mental list: *If it was Hans, where did he get the book? It was a relatively new children's book. He didn't buy it in town. When we made inquiries at the local Borders we got zilch; zero copies of "Little Boy Blue" were sold in the past week. And the previous search of his room gave no indication of his being a children's lit fan.*

Lois's ruminations were interrupted by the return of the ruddy-faced rookie. His quick head signal motioned her to the far end of the library where they could find some privacy. "Got it!—I think," he qualified. "I searched Hans's room and found three interesting items." To forestall any criticism from his superior, he quickly added, "Don't worry. I followed protocol and put them in evidence bags. Then I went into his Hummer. He had a small suitcase full of children's toys and stuff in it. I can't prove *Little Boy Blue* was there, but it sure smells like it."

The young cop was eagerness personified. His first big case and he had stumbled over what might be the clinching circumstantial evidence.

More than finding the possible secure place for the book, he had collected a cache of items to be tested. No traces of poison that he could see. But what was Hans doing with a plastic bowl, a small hammer, and a butter spreader tucked away in various drawers beneath his boxers and T-shirts? As separate items, these tools were not deemed important earlier. Now as a group, they could be seen as ingredients of a potential do-it-yourself poison kitchen.

Sandy concluded his report to Lois by unprofessionally blurting out his opinion so all could hear, "The lab knows what to look for. If traces of ricin are on any of these implements, they'll find them. If it walks like a duck and talks like a duck, then . . . if you know what I mean."

Hans pushed back his chair. He faced his colleagues. "I do know what you mean. I came here to write a book, just like all of you writers did, but the situation begged to be exploited."

Mary Beth turned white. Concurrent seismic shifts took place in her stomach and in her belief-system.

Hans looked at her. He understood instantaneously. "I'm confessing all right, but not to murder. What do you people take me for? I'm confessing to having used the not-so secret stairs to renew my, ahem, previous relationship with Marian. In the first twenty-four hours I was at Prince George House, I learned how to by-pass the central noisy staircase and use the hidden one to enter and leave Marian's room at will, her will, I might add." Hans looked at Mary Beth, who had turned from white to an angry red. "Sorry," he said, "I enjoyed our games, but 'A Man's A Man For A' That.' " He paused as if giving himself stage directions, "Not what your friend Bobby Burns had in mind, but . . . ."

Hans lowered his voice. In the room full of people, he spoke to only one. "Jokes aside, Mary Beth, ours is an interlude that should be extended. I want to tell you that I've cared enough to hurt you. I do regret that. I got carried away by the drama of the moment. That's what dramatists do, remember? Yes, I'm the one who piled the books in front of your door. You were asking for trouble with your amateurish investigations. Sooner or later you were going to get too close to someone's secrets. I thought you'd be better off nursing a twisted ankle than something more serious." Hans suddenly stiffened, realizing the implications of guilt in what he had just said at about the same time his audience did.

In one stage-trained moment, he pulled a black .9 mm Glock out of his pocket, twisted Sarah's arm behind her back, and pressed the gun against her flesh.

Stunned silence filled the room. Mary Beth's color started to change again. She got as far as blotch when Hans backed Sarah towards the door in what seemed like slow motion. Sarah was the first to understand what was happening. And she understood not as a victim, but rather as an author. "Clara, tell Herman I'll be O.K., and, for Pete's sake, take notes. Take notes now. Freeze frame each person." Her orders to Clara gave Tony enough time to assess the situation as Hans pushed Sarah out of the door into the rain. Tony made a running tackle at Hans's legs, knocking him down while taking Sarah out with the same tackle. Many screams were heard (and never admitted to later) as people imagined they heard shots fired. Lois and Sandy knew better, but drew their guns as they rushed Hans.

"Cuff him, Sandy, and be sure to read him his rights," Lois ordered. She turned to Tony. "You were brave, Tony, but don't ever do such a foolhardy thing again. You don't tackle an armed man who has taken a hostage. You endangered yourself and Sarah. Were you asking for 'death by cop?' "

"Oh, Tony," Mary Beth was ecstatic. I've always known how smart you are, but never realized how magnificent."

"Ladies, ladies, calm down. Look." Tony pointed. Sandy had retrieved the black dripping gun. It was now embellished with strangely spreading orange spots around the muzzle. "The minute Hans backed into the rain, I saw that he was carrying a plastic water-pistol. The orange tipping that's required by law to identify toy guns was beginning to show. I paint bikes and can spot a drip (both ways, Mary Beth) when I see one. I knew there was no real danger, except from cheap shoe polish."

Hans broke into Tony's explanation. "Don't expect me to apologize. The fates handed me the ricin beads. I had children's books, the simplest of carriers, in my car. I had toy guns, too, by the way. It was innocent enough; I was bringing the toys and books to my nieces and nephews. And Marian was here. It took me just a few minutes to put together the three ingredients of beads, book, and Marian to create the perfect plot. I staged it perfectly, too, down to the cat-button evidence I planted in the staircase. That's what I do."

Lois thought, *self-incrimination won't be enough to convict. He'll have the best lawyers. Hans's scenario could have been pre-meditated. What about motivation?* She had a thick file of the information Ernie had uncovered with computer assisted forensics. Severe problems were crashing the relationship between Hans and his agent. Lois knew from her conversation with Mary Beth that Hans saw Marian as the direct cause of these problems. *He sure had plenty of malice aforethought*, she decided. She added the damning news that was all over the Internet about Hans's career plummeting. She had a case. "It's murder one," she said quietly to Sandy.

Buck couldn't believe what Hans had said. For once he was almost stunned into jokelessness. He and Hans had been buddies. "I should have guessed," he said. "I know his reputation as a micro-manager in the theater. He blocked out scenes, supervised costuming and make-up. Who else here could have done all that? Apologies to you ladies," he added, looking at Mary Beth, Clara, and Sara, "but none of you has a clue how to really wear make-up. I should have known. I'll be kicking myself in the chaps for this the rest of my life. Good thing I stopped wearing spurs."

Clara, breathing hard and gasping, reached for Buck for support. She pulled herself together and looked at Sara. "You were right, Sara." She turned and faced the group, "Sara was right, everyone. Marian's corpse was speaking to us as eloquently as it could. We should have paid more attention."

Sara who was also standing, felt delayed shock. She sat down heavily. For once she was beyond speech.

Hans ignored both women and spoke to Buck. "Yes, Buck. Anyone could have done a little research and read about this house. It was built for alibis and rendezvous. The staircase you-all have mislabeled 'secret' is well-documented. Even your friend the bike salesman found it," he sneered.

"But you've been caught," Buck countered. "You know what we used to say around the campfire, 'Never was a horse that couldn't be rode; never a man who couldn't be throwed.' "

Hans wasn't listening. "She had it coming. If I hadn't helped her make her final grand theatrical exit, someone else would have. It had to be all Marian, all of the time. No more.

"But I did make her look great for her final curtain call, didn't I?" He smiled.

Mary Beth was visibly shocked. Tony moved to her side.

Her feeling of relief on finding Marian's murderer was unexpectedly complicated.

Hans reached out. Sara and Clara instinctively ducked. Mary Beth not previously known for her stand patism, didn't move. Hans's intense blue eyes held hers. He touched her gently on the shoulder in what, she thought, was meant as a farewell gesture.

Or was it?

The End

ABOUT THE AUTHOR

 **DR. AUDREY LAVIN** started her teaching and writing career with a B.S. from Northwestern University. She went on to earn her Ph.D. at Case Western Reserve University, where she also taught. Along the way, she has attended many writing conferences; murder may or may not have occurred. Lavin assures her readers that these conferences in the U.S. and in the fifteen countries (including Turkey) where she has taught were more civilized and less fun than the one she features in *Eloquent Corpse*.

Eloquent Corpse is Lavin's fifth book. It is the much-awaited sequel to *Eloquent Blood* and features some of the same amateur detectives with a new cast of eccentric victims and unlikely suspects.

Lavin lives in Canton, Ohio, with her consultant husband Carl and many visits from children and grandchildren. To learn more, go to her "Whodunit" blog at:

http://indianhillmediaworks.typepad.com/whodunit/

www.ingramcontent.com/pod-product-compliance
Lightning Source LLC
Chambersburg PA
CBHW031352170626
46807CB00002B/938